Hometown Love

Donuts, Books, and Jocks

Love Blooms In Cloverdale

Painted Love

Multiple Authors

Phoenix Voices Anthologies

Copyright © 2023 by Carol Cassada, Ireland Lorelei, MacKade

All rights reserved. No part of this publication may be reproduced, stored or transmitted in any form or by any means, electronic, mechanical, photocopying, recording, scanning, or otherwise without written permission from the publisher. It is illegal to copy this book, post it to a website, or distribute it by any other means without permission.

This novel is entirely a work of fiction. The names, characters and incidents portrayed in it are the work of the author's imagination. Any resemblance to actual persons, living or dead, events or localities is entirely coincidental.

Carol Cassada, Ireland Lorelei, MacKade asserts the moral right to be identified as the author of this work.

Carol Cassada, Ireland Lorelei, MacKade has no responsibility for the persistence or accuracy of URLs for external or third-party Internet Websites referred to in this publication and does not guarantee that any content on such Websites is, or will remain, accurate or appropriate.

Designations used by companies to distinguish their products are often claimed as trademarks. All brand names and product names used in this book and on its cover are trade names, service marks, trademarks and registered trademarks of their respective owners. The publishers and the book are not associated with any product or vendor mentioned in this book. None of the companies referenced within the book have endorsed the book.

Contents

Donuts, Books, and Jocks

Love Blooms In Cloverdale

Painted Love

Donuts, Books, and Jocks

By: Carol Cassada

Phoenix Voices Anthologies

Contents

Donuts, Books, and Jocks #

Donuts, Books, and Jocks

By: Carol Cassada

The morning sun rose over the Carolina town of Danburg. Residents would soon be waking for work and school. Daisy Foster hummed along to a Christina Aguilera tune on the radio as she meandered around the kitchen of Daisy's Delights, her donut shop. Her auburn hair was covered by a hair net while her tank top and apron were sprinkled with flour.

It was a busy week for Daisy. Not only did she have to prepare orders for the daily customers, but she had to make one hundred and fifty donuts for her class reunion. This weekend was Danburg High's ten-year reunion. It was a big affair and everyone was doing their part to make it a success. Although the order required a lot of work, Daisy didn't mind helping out.

After placing a tray of chocolate donuts into the oven, Daisy started working on the special batch for the reunion. She was actually looking forward to the event. Many of her classmates remained in Danburg and with it being a small town, she was always bumping into somebody. Yet, most of the students left after graduation, and hardly kept in touch.

Daisy was one of the few who still called the place home. She had a good life going in Danburg with her donut shop and wouldn't change it for anything.

After graduating from community college, Daisy worked as a baker at one of the big chain grocery stores. She was a whiz at all desserts, but donuts were her specialty. Although the job paid well, Daisy yearned to unleash her creativity in the kitchen instead of sticking with the bakery's menu. Soon she'd get an opportunity to do that with a little help from fate.

Mrs. Mosley, the beloved town donut baker, decided to retire and move to Florida after fifty years in the business. When her shop came up for sale, a light bulb went off in Daisy's head. This was the opportunity she was looking for. With her own bakery, she could build her brand and add new flavors to the donut world. After a lot of thinking and calculating, Daisy decided to take a chance on her dream. With the help of a bank loan, Daisy purchased the bakery and renamed it Daisy's Delights.

It was a risky investment, but a profitable one. Every day, customers came in for one of Daisy's sweet concoctions. She had the usual treats like glazed donuts and chocolate eclairs. But she liked to experiment with new ideas. Her peanut butter and chocolate donuts were a hit with kids, while adults couldn't get enough of her lemon crullers.

As soon as Daisy switched the sign to open, customers began arriving. A mom of two ordered a box of chocolate sprinkled donuts, then Mr. Beardsley came in for his daily glazed donut before heading to the library.

Daisy set a fresh batch of strawberry crullers into the display case when she spotted her friend Jennifer Mathers coming in. Jennifer wasn't acting like her chipper self and based on her messy ponytail and dark circles were under her brown eyes.

"What can I get for you?" Daisy cheerfully greeted her pal.

Jennifer gave her an annoyed look. "How about a time machine to go back and convince me not to volunteer for the reunion committee?"

"Sorry my time machine's in the shop."

"In that case, I'll take two cheesecake eclairs. Oh, and a box of jelly donuts."

"Strawberry, grape, or raspberry?"

"A little of each." Jennifer took a sip of her iced coffee, the refreshment offered a boost of energy. "I figured I'd drop them at the shop for Charlie. He's been a godsend during the reunion planning."

Daisy laughed as she fetched a box. Jennifer's husband Charlie was a classmate of theirs. He was known as the class clown and had everyone laughing with his puns. He and Jennifer seemed like an odd match with his laid back personality and her hyperness. Yet, they've been going strong after five years of marriage and a one-year old son who was just like his dad.

"How's the planning coming along?"

"I'll be glad when it's over." She rubbed the ache forming in her neck. "When it's time for our twentieth reunion, I'm staying away from the committee."

"Good advice." Daisy filled the pink box with four grape jelly donuts. "Are you expecting a big turnout?"

"We sent out invitations to all the classmates. Half of them RSVP'd, as for the others who knows."

"Well, I know of at least four people who'll be attending. You, Charlie, me and Ethan."

"Ethan's coming?"

"Yeah, I talked him into it. I swear if it wasn't for me, he'd have no social life."

Jennifer smirked took another sip of coffee as Daisy talked about Ethan. "Oh, I've got a secret to tell you. Don't breathe a word to anybody." She looked around the empty shop then motioned for Daisy to move closer. "Rumor has it Brock Tate is coming."

"No!" Daisy shouted, then immediately lowered her voice. "He'll be at the reunion."

"He RSVP'd, but whether he shows is a different story. With his busy schedule, I'm surprised he'd make time for us folks."

Brock was Danburg High's all-star basketball player who led the team to a championship. His amazing skills on the court lead to numerous offers from top colleges. Brock's success continued throughout college and by his junior year, scouts were interested in him. Every professional team wanted him and he got drafted to New York, where he was the star attraction.

"Do you think he'll show up?"

"Who knows?" Jennifer shrugged. "But this will be a great reunion with or without Brock."

***

"Good choice, Joel. This is one of my favorite R.L. Stine books." Ethan Galloway scanned the book, then glanced at the young boy who was excited to read the latest installment of the Goosebumps series.

In the day and age of technology, it made Ethan happy to see kids who loved reading. As a kid, Ethan found more excitement in escaping into a literary adventure than in video games. His love of reading earned him the reputation of being a dork by many classmates, but he didn't care.

Some people loved sports, others loved cooking, his passion was books. Now as a librarian, he was helping people find their next great read.

Ethan stamped the card, then handed the book to Joel. "The book is due back on the twelfth."

"Thanks Mr. Galloway."

"Happy reading." Ethan called out as Joel left.

Ethan glanced around at the other library patrons. A group of students gathered around a table, cramming in last-minute studying for finals. In the children's corner, a mother was reading a princess story to her daughters. Over in the lounge area, Mr. Beardsley was reading the newspaper like he did every day.

He took the rolling cart to put the books back on the shelves when he spotted Daisy coming up the sidewalk. He ran his fingers through his short curly hair, then smoothed his blue dress shirt.

Daisy entered, smiling with a James Patterson book in one hand and a paper bag in the other. "Hi Ethan," she whispered.

"I'm here to return my book and bring you a lemon cruller."

"Thanks Daisy!" He took the bag from her and placed it behind the counter. "I'll save it for lunch." He then took the book and scanned it. "What did you think of the story?"

"I'll save my opinion for book club."

Danburg Library had a book club that met on the first Thursday of every month. The group consisted of Ethan, Daisy, Mr. Beardsley, and four other members. They read a variety of books, everything from suspense to sci-fi to chick lit. Although some of the men didn't care for the romance genres, they read them anyway, and to their surprise enjoyed them.

"What book can I help you pick out this week?"

"I'm in the mood for romance. Maybe something contemporary."

"Follow me."

Daisy trailed behind as Ethan pushed the rolling cart. "I probably won't do much reading this weekend because of the reunion."

"I'm actually looking forward to it." He halted to put two books back on the shelves. "I'm glad you talked me into going."

"It'll be fun, just like the old days."

Ethan smiled as he thought about his school days at Danburg High. He transferred there when his was thirteen. Being a bookworm and somewhat of a brainiac, Ethan was deemed uncool by the popular kids.

He was shy and kept to himself, but one day he met the girl who would change his life. Ethan was coming out of the school library, juggling his binder and textbooks when he bumped into Daisy, who rounded the corner.

Ethan's books along with Daisy's papers went flying to the ground. He immediately scrambled to pick up the items, muttering his apologies. "I'm sorry, I wasn't looking."

"It's not your fault. I was distracted." Daisy handed him his math book while he returned her report on George Washington.

"Galloway, right?"

"I beg your pardon."

"You're Ethan Galloway, the new kid."

"Yes, that's me."

"I'm Daisy Foster." She shook his hand. "You're in my Algebra class. You sit two seats ahead of me."

"Oh, yeah. I remember." The first day of class as Ethan took his seat he recalled a girl with red brown hair smiling at him. He got butterflies in his stomach looking at her that day. Now here he was having a conversation with her.

"How do you like Danburg High so far?"

"It's nice. The teachers are great."

"Have you made any friends?"

"Well, well, look who it is." Alec Johnson, a star player from the football team approached them. "Daisy, why are you hanging out with this dweeb? You can do so much better." "Leave us alone, Alec," she ordered.

"Oh, you're into nerds. I guess you're not as cool as I thought you were." Alec's tall frame towered over Ethan, who held his composure. "What are you going to do four eyes?"

"Is there a problem here?" Charlie came strutting down the hall, dressed in jeans, a hot pink shirt, and lime green headbands and wrist bands. He had one arm wrapped around Jennifer, and his eyes were transfixed on the bully. "Are you messing with my friends, Alec?"

Alec glanced at Ethan, then back at Charlie. "You're friends with this geek too?"

"He's a nice kid." Charlie nodded at Ethan as if giving his approval.

"Charlie, I thought you were cool. But you're as big a nerd as him." Alec pointed to Ethan.

"You know what Alec." Charlie snapped his wristbands. "Instead of focusing on Ethan, you need to concentrate on your butterfingers, and I'm not talking about the candy."

Alec's lips pressed into a thin line at Charlie's insult.

"Your hands are more slippery than a ski slope," Charlie jokingly replied. "The only thing you're good at catching is a cold on test day."

Alex's hands trembled as he thought of a snappy comeback. "Up yours, Charlie."

Charlie pressed his hands over his chest while feigning shock. "That hurt, Alec."

Ethan watched as Alec stomped away in a huff. "Thanks man." He turned to Charlie.

"No problem." Charlie brushed off his shirt. "If he gives you anymore trouble, let me know." Ethan nodded.

"Ethan Galloway, I'd like you to meet my friends Charlie Mathers and Jennifer Yearns." Daisy smiled as Ethan shook Jennifer's hand and fist bumped Charlie.

"Any friend of Daisy's is a friend of ours." Charlie put his arm around Ethan.

That day the four of them became inseparable. Many friends lose touch after school, but Ethan was happy to have them in his life.

"This is my aisle." Daisy searched the shelves for a book that caught her eye.

"If there's a certain author you're looking for, let me know."

"Thanks Ethan."

He looked back at the checkout desk to see two college boys.

"Excuse me, I have some patrons to help."

Daisy watched as Ethan strolled to the counter with a pep in his step. He'd come a long way from the shy kid in school. As he grew older, he gained more confidence. But that wasn't the only thing that changed. He traded his glasses for contacts, and his curly hair was cut into a shorter do.

Ethan had good looks, smarts, and a kind heart. Daisy wondered why so lucky girl hadn't snatched him up yet. A small pang hit Daisy's stomach, she placed one hand on her abdomen and the other on the bookcase. When no other aches came she shrugged it off and continued gazing at the books.

Her thoughts shifted back to Ethan. In all the years she'd known him, he never had a steady girlfriend. He went on his share of dates, but none of them ever turned into a full-fledged relationship.

Maybe he hasn't found the right one. Daisy knew that feeling all too well. In the twelve years, she'd been dating, she had two serious boyfriends. There was Trent, her college boyfriend. The two bonded over their love for books and art. Daisy fell fast for him and thought he could be "the one."

However, after graduation, Trent broke up with her. He said he wanted to spread his wings and see what the world had to offer him. The last Daisy heard, he was managing a fast food restaurant in Florida.

Then there was Shawn, the gym instructor. Daisy met him when she attended a yoga class with Jennifer. While Shawn was handsome on the outside, he was ugly on the inside. The exercise buff began making snide comments about Daisy's onehundred-and-thirty-pound frame. "You need to lay off the donuts. If you hit the gym more, you could tone up your body."

Daisy wasted no time in giving Mr. Fitness instructor the heave ho. It'd been nearly two years since the Shawn debacle, and Daisy's remained single since then. She was taking her time when it came to jumping into the next relationship. When and if she did settle down, she wanted it to be with a nice guy, someone like...

Her concentration was cut short by two girls giggling, which was met by a shush from Ethan. Daisy picked a Debbie Macomber book, then waved to Ethan she was ready to check out.

"Did you find what you were looking for?"

"Yeah." She nodded, although her thoughts were still on her dating life.

"Alrighty. You'll all set." When he handed the book to her, his fingers brushed her knuckles, sending a tingling sensation up his spine.

"Thanks, Ethan." Daisy blushed at the touch of his fingers. "I need to get back to the shop. I'll see you on Saturday."

"Bye, Daisy." Ethan watched as she walked out the door. When he turned around he saw Mr. Beardsley standing before him, raising a white bushy eyebrow. "Can I help you Mr. Beardsley?"

"Actually, I'm the one who's going to help you."

"I beg your pardon."

"Ethan, tell her how you feel."

"I don't understand what you're saying." Ethan shooked his head as he tidied the desk.

"I may be old, but I recognize a man in love when I see it." He pointed his finger at Ethan. "You love Daisy."

Ethan went to protest, but Mr. Beardsley interrupted him. "I see the way you look at her. That's the same way I looked at my Wilma. My God rest her soul," he blew a kiss to the sky. "What are you waiting for, tell Daisy how you feel."

Ethan tapped his fingers on the desk. He didn't know his feelings for Daisy were so obvious. From the moment he met Daisy, he was mesmerized and believed she was the most beautiful girl in the world. Although he liked Daisy, he never acted on his crush. The main reason is fear she'd reject him and it'd ruin their friendship.

"Don't let fear hold you back," Mr. Beardsley spoke. "If I had let fear stand in my way fifty years ago, I never would've asked

Wilma to the dance. We would never have fallen in love, gotten married, and had two kids."

Listening to Mr. Beardsley's story, Ethan realized it was time to take a chance. This weekend at the high-school reunion, he'd tell Daisy he loved her.

***

Green and yellow streamers hung from the rafters while colorful spotlight and the music of Katy Perry filled the school gymnasium. Dressed in a black and white polka dot dress, and her hair in waves, Daisy entered the gym. As she walked around, she waved to some of her classmates and Principal Wheeler who hadn't changed much in ten years. The school authoritarian still proudly sported a bald head and rounded belly.

As she neared the refreshment table, she was stunned by the sight.

"Oh, my God." She looked at Charlie dressed in a lime green suit, while Jennifer opted for a yellow halter dress. "Jennifer, how could you let him out of the house like this?" Daisy tries to stifle her laughter.

"At least I got him in a suit." She sipped her punch.

"Honey, you know I like to stand out." He tugged on his jacket sleeves. "Besides, you have to admit I look good."

Jennifer tried hard to smile, but it was no use. Although Charlie could be a pain at times, he knew how to make her laugh.

"Speaking of good looking men in suits." Daisy pointed to Ethan in a gray suit and black shirt with tie.

"Hey guys." Ethan approached them. "Jennifer, you did an amazing job."

"Thanks Ethan."

"Glad you came." Daisy smiled at Ethan. "You look nice." She was used to seeing him in khakis or jeans with a dress shirt. But when it came to special occasions, he made a fashion choice.

"Watch out, Ethan. All these single ladies will be lining up for you." Charlie waved his finger around the room.

Ethan grinned at his friend's vote of confidence. While there were many gorgeous women here, Daisy was the one who had his heart. Later tonight he'd lay all his cards on the table and tell her how he felt. Hopefully, they'd walk out as a couple.

Throughout the evening, the foursome danced and mingled with their classmates. Many of the Danburg students went on to successful careers and raise families. Daisy's ear was talked off with Robbie Alderson bragging about law firm while Nicole Gentry showed off photos of her twin girls.

Daisy returned to the refreshment table where Ethan was indulging in her cream filled donuts with green and yellow icing.

"Another masterpiece." Ethan held up the half eaten donut.

"Thanks." She poured a glass of punch. "My donuts seem to be a hit with everyone."

"I've heard people raving about them when they weren't bragging about their five digit paychecks."

Daisy laughed. "I swear if I have to hear one more person talk about their Corvette or mega mansion, I'm going to scream."

"I know a way to work out you frustrations." Ethan wiped his hands on a napkin, then motioned toward the dance floor.

Daisy gestures for him to lead and followed him as a Lady Gaga song blared on the speakers. She moved her hips to the rhythm while Ethan's feet glided in a move reminiscent of the electric slide. She couldn't believe the moves on him.

"I think I have competition." He nodded to Charlie, whose dance moves made him look like a flailing arm inflatable.

"That's one person who'll never change," she quipped.

Gaga's Poker Face ended as Amazed by Lonestar began playing. Ethan and Daisy gazed at each other, waiting for the other to make a move.

This is it. Ethan held out his hand and Daisy took it. The two danced closely, goosebumps raised on Ethan from Daisy's touch and the smell of her lavender perfume.

Daisy kept her focus on her feet, but she couldn't help peering at Ethan. She didn't understand why she was nervous slow dancing with Ethan, they'd done it before.

"This brings back memories of our prom, remember."

Ethan nodded as he reflected on their senior prom. He wasn't planning on attending, but when Daisy bemoaned not getting a date and missing out, he jumped to her rescue. Ethan asked if she wanted to go with him — as friends of course.

Daisy immediately said yes, and Ethan tried to make the big night as special as possible. He rented a tuxedo and chipped in on a limo with Charlie and Robbie. He also splurged on a light pink corsage, which fit perfectly with Daisy's royal blue dress.

When he picked her up that evening, he was bowled over by her appearance. She looked gorgeous in the spaghetti strap dress with her hair swept into an elegant ponytail.

The prom was one of the most memorable moments for Ethan. He and Daisy danced all night, even during the slow songs. He was just as jittery as he was now. Looking back, Ethan kicked himself for not telling Daisy he loved her.

He might have missed his chance back then, but he wasn't going to let it slip his fingers again.

"Daisy, I...I have something to tell you." He glanced into her hazel eyes. "I..."

"Oh, my God! It's Brock Tate."

The music stopped and the crowd dissipated as Brock's six-foot, six inch frame came waltzing into the gym. He dressed neatly in a blue suit and white shirt, while his dark hair was trimmed into a buzz cut. Onlookers gaped and camera flashes filled the area as everyone tried to get a glimpse of the celebrity.

Daisy held onto Ethan's hand as they watched Brock stroll by them on his way to the stage.

"I can't believe he came," Jennifer whispered as she came up beside Daisy.

"This is a surprise." Daisy grinned at the sight of Danburg's most famous celebrity.

"Ladies and gentlemen," Principal Wheeler spoke into the microphone. "It's my pleasure to introduce one of Danburg High's best students and basketball players, Brock Tate."

The crowd erupted into cheers as Brock came up onstage. He hugged Principal Wheeler then grabbed the microphone from the stand. He paused to relish in the admiration shown from his classmates. After ten years away, he returned to Danburg as the biggest success story, an honor he was proud of.

When the applause died down, Brock spoke. "These days, I have a busy schedule being on the road for basketball. But when I received an invitation for my high-school reunion, I was determined to be here." Brock's speech was met with more cheers. "I have so many fond memories of Danburg and our great school. Basketball has always been my passion, but I had people saying I wasn't good enough or I'll never make it in the pros." A round of boos filled the area at the mention of Brock's naysayers.

"But thanks to the guidance of Coach Gibson..." he pointed to a gray-haired man to the side of the stage. "I got the confidence I needed. Thanks to him, my game improved and I helped lead

the Wildcats to a state championship."

"You're number one Brock," a man shouted.

Brock smiled before continuing his speech. "This school, the teachers, coaches, and students were an important part of my life. I'm happy to be back home celebrating with you all." More cheers erupted. "I think I've talked long enough, let's get back to the party."

The music restarted as Brock exited the stage. Immediately a crowd gathered wanting autographs and photos with the star.

Daisy, Ethan, and a few others kept their distance.

"If I had known he was coming, I would've brought my basketball for him to sign." Charlie's comment was met by an elbow nudge from his wife.

"Brock knows how to make an entrance." Ethan watched the jock savoring in the glory.

"He certainly does." Daisy admitted she was starstruck by Brock's arrival. But she wasn't going crazy like everyone else. Although Brock was now a big star, to her he was still a regular guy.

As Brock finished with the photos and autographs, he looked up and noticed a cute redhead near the refreshment table. She looked familiar, but with so many classmates it was hard to keep track of the names.

"Excuse me, ladies and gentlemen." He walked toward the table. He'd only been here ten minutes and already he was hungry. "I hope you folks don't mind if I hang out."

"Not at all." Charlie moved out of Brock's way so he could get some punch.

"You're Charlie Mathers, right?"

"Yes, that's me." Charlie beamed, honored that Brock remembered him.

"I remember during science class you picked up that frog and began singing Hello My Baby."

"Yeah, that was me."

"I thought that was hilarious."

"Mr. McCorkle didn't think so, I got detention." "Are you still the jokester?"

"Most definitely," Jennifer replied.

"Brock, I'd like you to meet my wife, Jennifer Yearns. She was a Danburg student."

"I apologize, your name doesn't ring a bell." Brock shook her hand. "Tell me, how do you manage to handle this guy?"

"It's not easy, I'll tell you that much." She put her hand on Charlie's shoulder, and looked up adoringly at him. "But he does make me laugh when I'm having a bad day."

Brock's attention then went to Ethan. "Galloway, right. Ethan?"

"Yes, sir." He shook Brock's hand, a bit awestruck that a star of his caliber remembered little folks like him.

"You were a lifesaver for me in English class." "It was nothing." Ethan shrugged.

"The heck it wasn't. If you hadn't tutored me on *Of Mice and Men*, I never would've passed and would've been kicked off the team. I owe you one man."

"I did what any good person would do."

"You don't find many people like him," Daisy replied.

Brock's gaze moved to Daisy, who looked more stunning now that he was closer. "And who is this lovely lady? Is it your girlfriend, Ethan?"

"No...no...she's my friend." Ethan felt awkward being put on the spot. Naturally, strangers would assume he and Daisy were a couple. But until he told Daisy he lover her, he had no right calling her his girlfriend.

"I'm Daisy Foster." She held out her hand. "Former classmate and proud Danburg resident." She felt foolish for laying on the cheerfulness too thick.

"It's a pleasure to meet you, Daisy."

"Did we have any classes together?"

"Mrs. Shayne's Algebra class. I sat in the front of the class, while you and the cool kids sat in the back." Throughout school Daisy was never one of the popular kids. Although she was pretty, smart, and involved in many activities; she never thought she fit in with the other kids.

"So what do you do now?"

"I'm a baker. I have my own donut shop."

"Really?" Brock was impressed. Daisy was a woman with beauty and brains.

"Yes, I made a batch of donuts for tonight." She motioned toward the platter, and Brock picked up the round pastry.

"I normally don't eat sweets, but one won't hurt." Brock bit into the donut and was overcome by the sweetness of the cream filling. "This is delicious."

Daisy didn't know if Brock was sincere, but she accepted the compliment.

Brock finished devouring the delicacy. "Time to burn off those calories." He listened to the upbeat music. "Daisy, care to dance?"

"Me?" She pressed her fingers to her chest.

"My fancy footwork isn't for the basketball court."

Daisy was awestruck that of all the women he asked her. She would be a fool to turn down the opportunity to dance with a famous celebrity.

"Let's go."

Brock ushered Daisy to the middle of the dance floor. Daisy tapped her feet while Brock waved his arms as the Justin Timberlake song picked up tempo.

Across the room, a dejected Ethan watched as the girl of his dreams was dancing with the famous jock. He felt like he was in school again. The awkward smart kid, who gets ignored for an athlete.

"Are you okay?" Charlie gently nudged Ethan's arm.

"Yeah, I think I'm going to go home."

"Why? The night's still young."

"I have a lot of errands tomorrow and want to get an early start." It was a lame excuse, but the best he could come up with.

"I'll catch up with you later."

Ethan walked toward the exit, but stopped to glimpse at Daisy one last time. His plan for a perfect evening with Daisy was disrupted by Brock.

***

With a large mocha latte at her disposal, Daisy needed all the caffeine she could for today. The excitement of last night gave her a restless night. But she mustered up enough energy for work. Danburg residents along with a few classmates would be filling in soon for donuts.

Daisy was quite popular last night, most of the attention was because of her donuts. But all eyes were on her because of Brock. It wasn't every day that a small town girl gets to dance with a celebrity. Although to her Brock was a regular guy.

After Daisy's dance with Brock, many women lined up for their chance with the hunky basketball star. Brock happily obliged with his elderly teachers who wanted to dance with their favorite student. But many of the younger women dragged him to the floor.

While Daisy had fun at the reunion, she was disappointed Ethan left so early. The evening wasn't the same without him there, and she didn't buy the excuse he told Charlie. Ethan always told her everything and he didn't mention any "errands" to her.

Something else had to be bothering Ethan. He was having fun at the reunion, then for him to leave abruptly and without saying goodbye was odd.

***

The sun peeked through the clouds as Ethan walked down the sidewalk. After arriving home last night, he immediately felt guilt for his behavior. He shouldn't have left so hastily, leaving Daisy worried. But the sight of her and Brock made his heart ache.

I'm an idiot. He mentally scolded himself. Brock's flirtation with Daisy had Ethan feeling inferior. A meekly librarian like him would never stand a chance against a professional basketball player.

Remember what Mr. Beardsley said. Ethan recalled the conversation with the elderly man. He couldn't let fear overcome him, especially now that Daisy's heart was on the line. He had to make his move.

Nearing the donut shop, Ethan breathed deeply before entering the store.

"Hi Ethan." Daisy smiled as she came out of the kitchen with a tray of Oreo donuts. She noticed he had a pep in this step, which meant he was in a good mood. "I missed you last night. Why did you leave so soon?"

"I wanted to go home to rest. I had errands to run today." Daisy arched an eyebrow at his response.

"Plus, I was starting to get a headache." He rubbed his forehead.

"Are you feeling better?" She didn't buy the excuse, and as much as she wanted to inquire about the real reason he left, she decided not to press the issue. If Ethan wanted to talk, she was there for him.

"Much better."

"An Oreo donut could brighten your day." She placed the tray on the counter for him to see.

"They look delicious. I'll take two for the road."

"Great."

Ethan pursed his lips as he watched Daisy. He couldn't put it off longer, although this wasn't how he imagined confessing his feelings, it was best to be straightforward. "Daisy, I need to tell you something."

She perked up at his comment. "What is it, Ethan? You can tell me anything."

He paused rubbing his hands on his jeans. This was it, the moment of truth. When he opened his mouth the bell over the door chimed, and Brock came striding in.

"Nothing like the smell of sweets to get you pumped up in the morning."

"Good morning, Brock," Daisy cheerfully replied.

"Morning Daisy. Ethan." He pulled Ethan into a handshake.

"We missed you last night Galloway."

"I'm sorry, I had to cut it short, but I have a busy day today." Ethan tried to hide his exasperation. Why was it that Brock managed to interrupt his chance to talk to Daisy. Was this fate sending him a message?

"You're up early. I figured all you celebrities slept in." Daisy teased.

"I've got a busy morning. The newspaper wants to do an interview, plus I'm meeting some pals for lunch."

"How about a donut to tide you over?"

"I'll take up the offer." Brock eyes the display case, licking his lips at the sweets. "I'll take a butter scotch and a glazed."

"Coming right up."

"Before I forget, I want to invite the two of you to a party on Tuesday at the community center."

"What type of party?"

"It's a welcome home party thrown by the town. I'd love it if you could come."

"Sure, I'll be there."

"Awesome." Brock turned to Ethan. "What about you?"

Ethan wanted to decline the offer and was about to when Daisy spoke.

"Come on Ethan. It'll be fun."

Looking at her big doe eyes, Ethan could refuse. "I think I'm free so I'll stop by."

"Great. You know this return home is shaping up to be something special." Brock flashed a dazzling smile at Daisy.

Ethan's stomach dropped at Brock's flirtation with Daisy. Of all the women, why did Brock have to take an interest in the woman Ethan loved.

"Here's your order, Ethan." She handed him the bag.

"Thanks Daisy." He handed her a couple of bills. "Keep the change." As he was leaving, Daisy called to him.

"Ethan, what were you going to tell me?"

He remembered he was getting ready to say, "I love you" before Brock came in. Ethan couldn't tell Daisy that, especially with Brock here.

"I wanted to know if you could make some eclairs for book club."

"Of course, I always bring donuts."

"Thanks Daisy," Ethan shyly replied. "I've got to get going, see you later.

"Bye Ethan," Daisy called out as he exited.

"Did he seem okay to you?" Brock watched Ethan walk away.

"He's just shy." Daisy shrugged, but she was concerned about Ethan. Earlier he made it seem like he wanted to discuss something important. But whatever it was, he didn't want to discuss it in front of Brock. *Maybe he'll tell me later.*

"I've got something to ask you, Daisy."

"Do you need me to make some donuts for the party?"

He giggled at her response. "Thanks for the offer, but we've got the food settled." He crossed his arms, then rested them on the display case. "I wanted to know if you wanted to go out to dinner."

The metal tray banged against the case, and almost flipped to the floor, but Daisy caught it in time. She was stunned by Brock's request and she thought she misunderstood him.

"Dinner?" She asked.

"Yeah, I thought we'd go to Isabella's Pizzas. What do you say?"

Her mouth went dry and her body felt limp. She grabbed the edge of the counter, hoping she didn't faint. The dance was one thing, but Brock was now asking her on a date. *It's not a date. It's dinner.* Just two former classmates catching up. But they did plenty of that during the reunion. Now Brock wanted one on one time with her.

She'd gone on plenty of dates before, but this one made her nervous. *Remember, he's just a regular guy. The same ole Brock.*

"What do you say, Daisy?"

"Okay," her voice cracked in response.

***

"It's not a date," Daisy spoke into the phone as she listened to Jennifer's hyper tone.

"Daisy, the world's most eligible, handsome, and famous basketball player wants to have dinner with you. Alone."

"It's just dinner, nothing else." Daisy put the phone on speaker as she finished cleaning the kitchen. "We're two friends catching up over a meal."

"As I recall, you and Brock weren't that close in school. But suddenly he's taken an interest in you."

Daisy rolled her eyes at Jennifer making a big deal over her dinner date with Brock. *Not a date,* she reminded herself. Although Daisy agreed with Jennifer's sentiment that Brock seemed interested in her. It was odd. Out of all the women, why her?

He's the type of guy who should be dating supermodels, not donut bakers. But maybe he was looking for someone not so high-maintenance.

"We're just friends, nothing more." Although part of Daisy did wonder what it'd be like to date a celebrity, she knew not to expect much from Brock. They were from different worlds, there's no way they'd work out. Could they?

"I want all the details. Let's meet tomorrow for lunch at Taco Casa."

"Alright. I'll see you tomorrow." Daisy said her goodbye, then hung up. Glancing at the time, she saw it was twenty minutes to seven. Almost time for dinner with Brock.

She finished cleaning the counters, then turned out the lights. She switched the sign to Closed and locked up for the night. Stepping outside, a light breeze broke the warmth of the May evening.

Daisy took a moment to take in the scenery. Danburg's spring night life was in full-swing. Customers were converging on The Frozen Dairy for a cold treat to combat the heat. In the nearby park, cheers could be heard from parents cheering on their kids' Little League game.

Danburg offered something for everyone, one of the perks Daisy loved about the town. She had a good life in Danburg, well almost perfect.

She walked down the street, her eyes focused on the Danburg Public Library in the distance. The place was closed, but in the morning Ethan would have it bustling. Daisy grinned as she thought of Ethan. He was one of the few people she knew that took pride in their work.

While she admired Ethan for his dedication to promoting literacy, she felt his life was too focused on work. Ethan's routine involved going to work then going home to an empty house with his books. With the exception of invites from Daisy, Jennifer, and Charlie; Ethan rarely was social. He needed to get out more, socialize, and find him a nice, decent woman to...Daisy was so deep in thought she bumped into a patron on the sidewalk.

"I'm sorry." Daisy looked at the college boy, who was holding a basketball jersey in his hands.

"If you want an autograph or a picture, I suggest you get in line."

Daisy looked past the young man at the crowd gathered around Brock outside of Isabella's Pizzas. People from all ages were holding out memorabilia or the phones hoping to get a moment with the basketball player.

Brock looked up from a hat he was signing to smile at Daisy. He motioned for her to go inside while he finished with his fans.

Daisy excused her way through the mob and entered the pizzeria. Bright lights reflected off the restaurant's red and white checkered floor, while photos from the restaurant's 1980 grand opening hung on the walls.

Rosa Moretti, the restaurant's manager and Isabella's granddaughter greeted Daisy. Her dark hair was pulled into a braid, and she wore her usual uniform of jeans and a red shirt with the restaurant's logo.

"Daisy, so glad to see you." Rosa pulled a menu from the podium. "Table for one."

"Actually, I'm meeting someone, but he might be a while." Daisy glanced out the window and the crowd was slowly diminishing.

"It's great to see Brock back," Rosa replied. "But some of these people are ridiculous with the way they treat him." She placed a fist on her hip as she watched the scene outside. "I swear, they're like vultures. As soon as he crossed the street, people were following him. I don't know how he puts up with it."

"I guess it's one of the things celebs have to deal with." Daisy glimpsed once more at Brock, who was smiling throughout the session. She admired him for keeping his patience, if she was in his shoes, she'd go crazy with the attention.

"I got a booth in the back to give you and him some privacy."

Daisy followed, and slid into the bench near the wall so she could have a view of Brock when he came in. After ordering an iced tea, Daisy skimmed the menu, her stomach grumbling with the thoughts of hot pizza and spaghetti. She was so entranced by the images of food that she didn't notice Brock until he slid into the booth.

"Sorry about that."

"It's fine." She waved her hand. "I guess you're used to it."

"It can be..." he rubbed his fingers together, trying to find the right word, "annoying at times. Especially the people who only want autographs to sell on eBay. But I don't mind interacting with the true fans."

"I bet you're starving after your autograph and photo session."

"Darn right." He glanced at the menu. "How would you like to split a pepperoni and sausage pizza?"

"Sounds good to me."

"Awesome. Would you like any pasta or salad?"

"Pizza will be fine with me."

When the waitress arrived, Brock ordered the pizza along with a bowl of baked ziti, and a Diet Coke. After their order was complete, talk turned to Brock's life in New York.

"It's a big city, always bustling with lots of activities."

"It seems like a great place to visit."

"If you ever decided to visit, I'd be happy to show you around."

Daisy nearly spewed her tea hearing his suggestion. Was he already envisioning a future for them?

"Thanks for the offer. But I don't know if I'll be able to visit anytime soon. I've got my donut shop to run. Plus, you've got a busy schedule and are on the road."

"I can always make time for a beautiful woman."

Daisy was caught off guard by his flattering comment, she didn't know how to respond, but luckily the food arrived before she could speak. The first few minutes were silent as they delved into their food, then in between gulps of baked ziti, Brock inquired about Daisy's job.

"How did you get into baking?"

"It started in home ec class." She picked a piece of pepperoni from her plate. "I was a whiz at cooking, but baking was my forte. It became my passion. I loved experimenting and baking desserts for my family." Daisy went on to explain her journey to opening the donut shop.

"That's incredible. You should be proud of yourself."

She smiled and nodded. "I took a big risk."

"I love a woman who knows what she wants and goes for it." Brock winked

Daisy blushed and felt she would faint if Brock kept up with his flirtations. She was used to guys hitting on her, but Brock was taking his pickup lines to a new level.

"You're also someone who took big risks." She tried to steer the conversation away from her. "Not many people make it in professional sports, but luck was on your side."

"It takes more than luck." He broke off a piece of his crust. "I've loved basketball since I was a kid. I remember watching the games with my dad and thinking I wanted to be like those players." He dipped the bread in the marinara sauce from the ziti. "I admit I wasn't the best player, I couldn't hit a basket. But with practice and encouragement from my dad, and the coach, I improved my skills."

"Did you ever think you'd make it to the big league?"

He shook his head. "That was my dream, but I understood it was a long shot. That's why I majored in marketing as a backup plan. But before college graduation, I declared for the draft. Imagine my surprise when my name was called during the first round."

"Your hard work paid off." Daisy twirled the straw in her sweet tea. "You have everything you want."

"Not everything." Brock leaned back, while maintaining eye contact with Daisy. "I still haven't found the right woman."

Daisy's stomach did flip flops. Brock was laying it on thick with the flirting, while she was flattered, she was also nervous. If she didn't get out of her soon, she worried she might lose control.

"Are you ready for the check?" the waitress asked as she approached the table.

"Yes," Daisy replied.

Brock was stunned by her hastily reply. "Don't you want any dessert?"

"I'm fine, besides I'm full." She patted her stomach for effect. "Besides I need to get home to rest. I've got a big day of baking tomorrow."

Brock paid the check, then he and Daisy divided up the leftover pizza. Being the gentleman he was, Brock escorted Daisy back to the shop so she could get her car. Daisy's nerves were still high as Brock closely walked beside her. The smell of his aqua cologne hit her nose, sending tingles throughout her body.

She had to admit, everything about Brock was attractive, and she swooned at being in his presence. Yet, his hints about taking their relationship further had her jumpy. This was their first d...dinner and he was already thinking about a future. A relationship and marriage was the farthest thing from Daisy's mind, especially one with Brock. After her last breakup, she decided to take time for herself. Although she'd love to have a husband and kids one day, she wanted to make sure it was with the right man.

Reaching her Corolla, Daisy pulled her keys from her pocket, then turned to face Brock. "Thank you for a wonderful time."

"The pleasure is all mine." He smiled showing off his dazzling white teeth.

"I guess I'll be seeing you Tuesday at the community center."

"Who knows, you may see me before then."

Daisy's pupils dilated with the statement. *Is he asking me out on another date? What do I tell him?*

"I'll be stopping by the donut shop to pick up some sweets."

"Of course. We've got plenty to choose from." Daisy mentally admonished herself for being a fool. After her awkward behavior tonight, she figured there was no way Brock would still be interested in her. "Well, I better be heading home."

She turned toward the driver's side when Brock stopped her. "Hold on, Daisy."

She gazed into his brown eyes that were fixated on her. He slowly leaned forward and brushed a kiss on her cheek.

"Have a good night." He smiled before heading off in the opposite direction

Daisy felt her cheek, which was still warm from his lips. Fumbling with the keys, she unlocked the door. She placed the styrofoam box on the passenger side, then leaned back in the driver's seat.

Brock's kiss was an unexpected twist. Daisy's heart raced at the feel and thought of his touch, but her head and her gut were telling a different story. Tapping her fingers on the steering wheel, Daisy's mind wandered to Brock. Any woman would go bonkers if someone like Brock Tate kissed them, yet Daisy was calm. Although it was a shock and felt nice, it did little to excite her.

***

Normally Ethan would be chipper in the mornings, but the librarian was experiencing the Monday blues like many of the patrons. His plans for the weekend went bust thanks to Brock. It was obvious Brock was infatuated with Daisy and vice versa. Ethan's heart ached at the thought of losing the woman he loves to another man.

Throughout Sunday evening, Ethan began thinking about Daisy. He loved her and always would, but maybe the universe was sending a message. Maybe he and Daisy were destined to be a couple. Maybe they were destined to remain friends.

Ethan rolled the cart back to the desk when he heard Mr. Beardsley calling him. His wrinkled hand motioned for the librarian to come into the lounge area.

"Can I help you with anything Mr. Beardsley?" Ethan asked in a low voice.

"I wanted to know how did things go with Daisy."

Ethan winced as he recalled letting Mr. Beardsley in on his plan. After hearing Mr. Beardsley's story about how he met his wife, Ethan go the inspiration of how to tell Daisy of his feelings. Unfortunately, Ethan didn't have the same success as the elder man did with his wife.

"I didn't tell her."

"What?!" Mr. Beardsley's outburst caused other patrons to look in his direction. He apologized, then whispered. "Why didn't you tell her? You had it all planned."

"Well, my plans changed."

"What happened?"

Ethan's gaze fell to the newspaper sprawled across Mr. Beardsley's lap. The front page had a huge photo of Brock dressed in a suit, standing in front of the Welcome to Danburg sign. Everyone was fawning over Brock since his return, and Ethan was jealous of all the attention Brock commanded.

Mr. Beardsley followed Ethan's stare, it took his old mind a few moments before he connected the dots. "Let me guess, Mr. Basketball star put the moves on your woman."

"She's not my woman," Ethan slightly raised his voice, which earned an eyebrow raise from a woman looking at the newspaper stand.

Mr. Beardsley patted the seat next to him and Ethan accepted the gesture. "You can't let Brock swoop in and steal Daisy."

"It's not that easy."

"The hell it isn't. You need to fight for your woman."

Ethan wasn't a fighter, he didn't like arguments or physical violence. He steered clear of drama because he didn't want that in his life. As much as he disliked the thought of Brock with Daisy, if she wanted to be with him, Ethan wouldn't stand in her way.

"Mr. Beardsley, I appreciate you advice. But Daisy and I would never work out."

"You don't know that. You haven't even tried."

"Maybe I don't want to know."

"That's a lie. I know you love her and she feels the same."

"You don't know how she feels." Ethan understand Mr. Beardsley was trying to help, but his matchmaking skills were becoming an annoyance.

"I want you and Daisy to be happy." Mr. Beardsley folded the newspaper and cast it aside. As a friend and neighbor of the

Galloways and Fosters, he'd known Ethan and Daisy since they were kids. He remembered every morning he and Wilma would sit on the porch, drinking their coffee and waving to Ethan and Daisy as they passed by. When Wilma died two years ago, Daisy and Ethan were there for him. They'd stop by nearly every day with food or to check on him. Now he wanted to do something to help them.

"We will be happy," Ethan said with conviction. "Daisy will have a great life with Brock in his mega mansion and he'll lavish her with diamonds. As for me..." Ethan paused as he reflected on the differences between him and Brock. Any woman would choose the handsome, rich athlete over the librarian. "I'll find someone."

"But it won't be Daisy."

Ethan wanted to rebuttal, but he spotted two customers coming in. "I don't have time to talk, I need to get back to work." He was glad for the distraction because he was tired of discussing and thinking about his love life.

***

The shade from the umbrella shielded Daisy from the sun as she sat on Casa Taco's outdoor patio. She nursed an iced tea and read her romance novel while waiting for Jennifer. Her friend texted to say she'd be five minutes later. Daisy didn't mind, it gave her plenty of time to catch up on her reading. However, every so often her mind wandered to Brock.

She thought about the kiss last night. It was odd she felt zero enthusiasm over his show of affection. *What's wrong with me?*

"Sorry, I'm late." Jennifer plopped in the chair across from Daisy, then set her large tote on the concrete patio. "My eleven o'clock appointment didn't arrive till ten minutes after. Then she was fretting over her haircut. She wanted a simple trim, but complained I was taking too little off." She let out an exasperated breath, then flagged down the waitress to order a diet soda. "But enough about me. Let's talk about you."

Daisy closed her book, then set it aside on the table. "There's not much to discuss."

"Don't be modest." Jennifer arched her trimmed eyebrow. "You had dinner with Brock. Tell me everything that happened, don't skip the details."

"Well, we met at Isabella's Pizzas. Although Brock was late because autograph hounds were mobbing him outside the restaurant."

"Tell me about it. The other day, I saw him leaving Joe's Deli, and two boys were waiting outside, wanting a picture with him." Jennifer opened the menu and glanced at the lunch specials. "Go on."

"It was a nice evening. We discussed our lives and careers. When it was time to leave, Brock escorted me to my car and he..." Daisy's pause had Jennifer looking up from the menu,

anticipation filling her tan skin. "He kissed me." "He kissed you?" Jennifer's jaw dropped.

Daisy did a whispering motion, but luckily nobody was around to hear them. "It wasn't on the lips, it was on the cheek. Short and simple."

The waitress returned with Jennifer's drink, and Jennifer told her they'd need a few minutes before they ordered. Although Jennifer was starving, the only thing she was craving was more details about Daisy and Brock's kiss.

"How was it?"

Daisy chewed on her bottom lip, she should've said it was fantastic and she saw fireworks, but she couldn't lie. "It was nice."

Jennifer squinted her eyes. "Nice? That's it?"

"What do you want me to say?"

"I expected more emotion from you. It's not everyday a woman gets kissed by a celebrity."

Daisy knew Jennifer would find the kiss thing weird. The problem is Daisy didn't know how to explain it either. She admitted Brock was a good looking guy, but there was nothing there. "That's the thing. I figured I'd be more excited. My heart was racing a bit, but other than that I felt nothing."

"What do you mean nothing? Is Brock a bad kisser?"

Daisy shook her head. He was gentle and tender when he went in for the kiss. Like any woman, she should've turned to jelly and crave more. But nothing. Nada. Zippo.

"I didn't feel a spark or a connection between us."

"Were you hoping for a spark?"

"Brock's a nice guy, but..."

"He's not what you're looking for."

"I know it sounds silly. He has everything a woman wants, looks, an established career, and money. But it doesn't interest me."

"Honey, there's nothing wrong with that." Jennifer twirled the straw in her soda. "People have different ideas for what they want in a significant other. Take me for instance. I love a guy with a sense of humor."

Daisy side-eyed Jennifer's comment about Charlie.

"Okay, sometimes Charlie's jokes are corny, but he always makes me smile. Whenever I have a bad day, he cheers me up and I forget about my problems. He always tells me, life is meant to be fun instead of worrying."

Watching Jennifer light up while gushing about Charlie made Daisy crave that kind of love. She hoped one day she could find a guy as wonderful as Charlie. But one thing was certain, Brock wasn't that guy. She needed to put an end to their budding romance before things became serious.

***

A who's who of Danburg citizens filled the community center on Wednesday night. A huge banner hung from the ceiling welcoming Brock home. The buffet table was filled with an eclectic mix of food from the town's best restaurants. Mini subs, egg rolls, and cheesy Parmesean bread lined the tables.

Daisy rushed over to the community center after closing the shop. She was hoping to have a few minutes to talk to Brock. Since their dinner, he hadn't stopped by the shop like he promised. Daisy wished he would've that way she would've gotten this important discussion out of the way.

She hated the idea of breaking Brock's heart, he was a good man and he deserved love. But Daisy wasn't the woman for him. He might be upset at first, but over time he'd find the right girl.

Daisy scanned the room Brock, but didn't see him. She was second-guessing her decision to break up with him tonight. *It's a big night for him. Maybe this can wait til another day.*

"Penny for your thoughts."

A startled Daisy looked up to find Ethan standing beside her. "You snuck up on me."

"I didn't mean too. It looked like you were deep in thought."

Daisy didn't want to bore him with details about her and Brock. Her mind skimmed for an excuse, and came up with a simple one. "I had a long day at work, so I'm a bit tired."

"If you're tired, why don't you go home."

"I'm fine, besides I had a soda so I should be good to go." She gave a thumbs-up, yet Ethan eyed her suspiciously.

"Maybe some of this delicious food would help too." He ushered her to the buffet and Daisy's eyes widened at the assortment of goodies.

"I'm glad you came tonight." Daisy took the plate Ethan offered her. "You need to get out of the house more often."

"Work keeps me busy, and sometimes I'm bit of a homebody. But thanks to you, I'm getting out of my routine."

Daisy stopped munching on her cheese bread as she thought of Ethan's statement. The only time Ethan went out is when

Daisy convinced him. Even tonight, Ethan probably would've went straight home after work, but he's here enjoying the festivities. She didn't realize what a huge influence she was on Ethan.

"Ethan, there you are." Mia Pearson worked her way through the crowd. It wasn't hard to miss the petite, curvy burnette whose figure was hidden behind a flowy orange dress. Mia was a former classmate and a teacher at the elementary school.

"Hi Mia. I didn't know you were going to be here."

"Well, I wouldn't resist being here to help welcome home the town's hero." Mia smoothed a wrinkle in her dress. "I'm surprised you're here, Ethan. Usually, you're a homebody."

"Daisy convinced me to attend."

Mia flashed a smile in Daisy's direction. "I should've known. When one of you is out in public, the other isn't too far behind."

"We've always been as thick as thieves." Daisy sipped on her punch as she watched Mia lay on the charm. Compared to Mia, Daisy considered herself a five, while Mia was a ten. Mia was gorgeous and smart; which is why men fawned over her.

"You must be excited."Ethan nibbled on a tortilla chip.

"Summer break starts next week. Got any plans?"

"That's why I wanted to speak to you. I need to run an idea by you. Can we talk in private?"

Realizing she was the third wheel, Daisy excused herself.

"Take your time, I'll be over there."Daisy walked toward a line of chairs next to the windows, but glanced back at Mia and Ethan. Her stomach muscles tightened as Mia's fingers patted Ethan's arms. Suddenly, Daisy wasn't so hungry.

She took a seat and tried to ignore Mia and Ethan. But every so often she gazed in their direction. The duo was engaged in a serious conversation, and Daisy's mind wondered what was the topic.

"Mind if I sit down?"

Daisy's focus switched from Ethan to Patricia Lemons, the town's newspaper reporter. Patricia was glammed up for the event in a purple pantsuit, but opted for Skechers slip-ons instead of heels.

"Please by all means." Daisy motioned to the empty seat.

Patricia sighed as she sat. "It feels good to get off my feet. Ever since Brock returned, my boss has had me busy tracing his every move." She cradled her white leather handbag in her lap, then pulled out a pen and notebook. "I'm a journalist not a Daisy laughed at Patricia's comment. As a reporter for The Danburg Post for twenty years, Patricia was just as famous for her work as her big, blonde eighties hair. When it came to the happenings around Danburg, Patricia knew all the gossip.

"Brock's return has certainly turned heads."

"You've got that right." Patricia flipped open her small notebook. "Oh, I have you heard the latest gossip about Brock."

"What gossip?" Daisy knew she shouldn't be fishing into information about Brock, yet like everyone her interest was piqued upon hearing the juicy word.

"Rumor has it, he's been getting chummy with a lovely Danburg lady."

Daisy felt her body go limp. Her dinner with Brock was making the rounds across Danburg. It shouldn't be no surprise, everyone was bound to see them at Isabella's Pizzas. While Brock might be used to gossip, Daisy was horrified at the prospect of people whispering and inquiring about her personal life.

"Word is he was flirting with Candice Harvey."

Daisy did a double take at Patricia's information. *He and Candice. No it couldn't be. Could it?* "Are you sure?"

Patricia nodded. "I heard from several people who said he was at the Rustic Saloon on Sunday night, flirting with the blonde bartender."

Daisy's head buzzed as she reeled in the news. If what Patricia said was true, then that means Brock went to the bar after his date with her. During dinner, he laid on the charm with talk showing her the sights in New York. Then of course there was the kiss at the end of the evening. Brock's behavior had Daisy believing that he was interested in her. But why would he flirt with Candice hours after his date with Daisy.

As Daisy reflected the situation, she realized this was the reason Brock didn't come to the shop. *He's avoiding me.* Maybe Daisy's nervous behavior scared him off.. Or maybe he was feeling guilty and didn't want to face her. Either way, Daisy's notion that her and Brock shouldn't be a couple was confirmed.

***

"Ladies and gentlemen, may I have your attention, please." The room quieted as Mayor Lovett spoke into the microphone. "This has been an exciting week for Danburg. One of our famous residents Brock Tate came for a visit."

Applause filled the area as Mayor Lovett gestured to Brock, who was acting modest at the attention.

"As many of you know Brock was a star athlete on Danburg High's basketball team. Now he's taking his talent to the courts of New York and everywhere around the world. Even though he's got a busy schedule, this young man hasn't forgotten his roots. Tonight, we're here to honor this exceptional man."

More cheers erupted as Mayor Lovett hugged Brock and encouraged him to say a few words.

"Thank you for that introduction, Mayor Lovett." Brock cleared his throat. "Everyone thank you for coming tonight and for making my trip a memorable occasion. It's been wonderful seeing old friends, neighbors, and teachers. As I think back on life, Danburg was a huge part of making me the person I am." He pulled the microphone from the stand and began pacing. "This is a tight-knit community, who is always helping each other. Now I want to return the favor."

Brock motioned to a man on the side who came out carrying a giant piece of white paper.

"I am donating fifty-thousand dollars to help the Danburg community." Brock took the giant check from his assistant and flipped it around for everyone to see.

Cheers and shouts of "thank you, Brock" packed the space as photographers clamored for a photo. Mayor Lovett arose from his seat for a photo with Brock. The two men shook hands and the mayor smiled at the financial windfall.

"Brock, I speak for everyone when I say this is a surprise." Mayor Lovett gripped the young man's shoulder. "You're one of a kind, Brock. You're a role model, someone people should look up to."

"He's laying it on thick," Patricia whispered, and Daisy giggled at her observation.

"I can assure you, this money will be put to good use."

Patricia and Daisy glanced at each other, and rolled their eyes.

Mayor Lovett was only in his first term, yet he hadn't made any of the promises from his campaign. Potholes still filled the streets, while taxes continued to increase instead of decrease.

"As a sign of my gratitude, I hereby declare today Brock Tate day." The mayor's announced caused more applause along with shouts of "yes."

"Thank you, Mayor Lovett for this incredible honor. And thank you to everyone whose made this trip a special occasion." Brock pressed his hand to his heart to show his affection. "I think Mayor Lovett and I have talked enough for tonight. So let's relax, celebrate, and enjoy the fun."

Throngs of reporters immediately gathered around Brock and the mayor, while citizens anxiously awaited their chance to shake Brock's hand.

"When it comes to getting the audience's attention, Brock has Mayor Lovett beat."

Daisy turned to find Ethan had snuck up beside her. When Brock and Mayor Lovett's speech began, Ethan was still with Mia. She faintly smiled at seeing that Ethan was alone. "What did Mia want to discuss?"

"Oh, she wanted to partner with the library to encourage summer reading to her students. I told her I'd come up with some ideas."

Daisy faintly smiled, although she admired Ethan's dedication to helping children read, she couldn't help but be skeptical. Was Mia's plan solely for the children? Or was the teacher using it as a way to get closer to Ethan?

"Speaking of, where's Mia? Did she leave already?"

"She's over there." Ethan pointed to the group of people behind the reporters.

Mia fluffed her hair and smoothed her dress as she waited her turn to meet Brock. Seeing Mia plotting her move on Brock didn't spark any jealousy in Daisy. The donut show owner didn't care if Mia dated Brock, they'd probably be more compatible. But when it came to Mia cozying up to Ethan, Daisy's heart wrenched.

***

The next morning, Daisy was up at the crack of dawn working on batches of donuts. Baking was more than a career for Daisy, it was also an outlet. Whenever she was feeling stressed, she'd put on an apron and head to the kitchen. Mixing and kneading the dough provided her an outlet to forget about her problems.

Daisy wanted to forget about last night. First there was the gossip that Brock was a ladies man. Although Daisy knew she and Brock could be nothing more than friends, hearing the news that he was flirting with Candice was a shock. Brock's behavior made Daisy believe she was the only woman for him. But as she watched him interact with some of the other ladies last night, she wondered if he pulled the same act with him.

While Brock being a playboy didn't upset her as much as Ethan with Mia. She knew it was silly getting agitated over the two, but Daisy couldn't help it. Mia was a good person and a great teacher. Everybody loved her. As one of Danburg's eligible single ladies she could have her pick of any guy. Except for Ethan.

Mia was laying on the charm thick last night, it was part of her Southern upbringing. When she started talking and batted her eyelashes, men went weak. *Is Ethan one of them?*

Daisy shook her head at the thought. Aside from books, Mia and Ethan weren't compatible. Ethan deserved someone who was kind, smart, and a good cook, someone...

The timer dinged and Daisy pulled the tray of eclairs from the oven. It was the special batch for book club as per Ethan's request. She set them on the cooling rack, then pick up a tray of glazed donuts to take to the display case.

As Daisy restocked the case, the bell rang above the door. She looked up to see Jennifer enter with her five-year-old son Ryan by her side. Ryan was a perfect mix of Jennifer and Charlie. While the boy had his mom's blonde hair and blue eyes, he inherited Charlie's sense of humor.

"Aunt Daisy, guess what?" Ryan happily exclaimed.

"What is it little man?" She bent so she was eye level with the youngster.

"Brock is going to be at school today."

"He is." Daisy's gaze shot up to Jennifer, who nodded.

"They're having a big assembly and he's talking to the students. Rumor has it, he also has a surprise for them."

Daisy mouthed "wow" at Jennifer's declaration. If Brock was hoping for a relaxing trip, he wasn't getting it. Yet, Daisy suspected he secretly loved the attention and being treated like a celebrity.

"Ryan's looking forward to this. So I figured for the big day, I'd give him a treat."

"Mom, can I have chocolate chip donut?" he tugged on his mom's hand.

"Yes, sweetie." She handed Daisy a five dollar bill. "One chocolate chip donut and some milk please."

Daisy handed the donut and the small bottle to Ryan.

"Thank you, Aunt Daisy."

"You're welcome, sweetie."

"Honey, why don't you sit and eat, while I talk to Aunt Daisy." Jennifer watched Ryan settle into a nearby chair and immediately dig into his donut. "Speaking of Brock, have you had a chance to talk to him?"

"No, I haven't. I was planning on talking to him last night, but didn't get a chance."

Jennifer nodded, then sipped on the coffee from her travel mug. News of Brock's generosity spread like wildfire around Danburg. "Daisy, you need to talk to Brock. Let him know there can be nothing between you. But remember to do it gently." "I don't think I have to worry about breaking his heart.

"What do you mean?"

"According to Patricia, Brock was spotted getting cozy with Candice Harvey late Sunday evening."

"That jerk!" Jennifer's exclamation caused Ryan to look up. "Sorry, honey. Finish your donut." The boy didn't give it a second thought as he devoured the remainder of the treat. "I can't believe he's a two-timer. But then again what do you expect from a celebrity."

"Jennifer, it's no big deal."

"No big deal." She placed her bangle decorated wrist on her hip. "He was pulling on the charm with you, making you believe he was interested. Then he goes and makes a move on Candice. Girl, I'm sorry."

"Don't be." Daisy wiped crumbs from the counter. "I mean, at first I was upset. Then the more I thought about it, the more I calmed. As I said, there was no spark between me and Brock, and I can't see us in a relationship."

"You're taking this a lot better than I would."

Daisy smirked. She wondered what Jennifer's reaction would be if Charlie ever cheated, something Daisy was guaranteed would never happen. Charlie adored Jennifer and had a good life with her, he'd be an idiot to break her heart.

"Brock's not the guy for me, but there's another man out there."

***

With his assistant taking over the front desk, Ethan tidied up the reading corner for book club. By nighttime, the library was fairly quiet with the exception of a few students cramming in study sessions. Ethan set the chairs in a circular pattern, then fetched a pitcher of tea from the refrigerator in the break room.. Usually, he served coffee for the book club, but with the weather getting warmer, he thought tea would be a nice change of pace.

As Ethan set up the refreshments, he spotted Mia coming toward him. "Hey Mia, you're early." Ethan glanced at his watch. "Book club doesn't start for another fifteen minutes."

"I won't be staying for book club. I have a date."

"It's no problem." Although most members attended rain or shine, there times when they had to skip the meetings. "You can give us your thoughts during the next meeting."

"Thanks Ethan." Mia grinned at how understanding Ethan was. "The reason I stopped by is to discuss our idea for the children's summer reading."

"I've been thinking it over." Ethan set a stack of napkins next to the pitcher and paper cups. "A rewards program is a good way to get children interested in reading."

"I'm glad you're on board. Now we need to think of what type of rewards to give them."

"I've got some ideas on that." He removed his glasses and clipped them to his shirt collar. "What if we do something simple like, a free donut from Daisy's Delights, a free slice of pizza from Isabella's Pizzas, or a free scoop of ice cream from The Frozen Dairy."

"That sounds wonderful. Do you think the owners will agree to it?"

"I know Daisy won't mind. As for the others, I'm sure they'll hop on board when I tell them it's for a good cause."

"Thank you, Ethan. You don't know how much this means to me."

"I do have some other ideas about library events for the kids."

"That'd be awesome." The binging of Mia's phone interrupted their conversation. She held up her finger to excuse herself, then checked the message. "Ethan, if you don't mind, can we discuss this later. I have to meet my date."

"No problem. Stop by sometime next week and we'll discuss it."

"Thank you again, Ethan." She clasped her hands in a grateful manner. "Be sure to tell me what the next book club pick is."

"Will do." Ethan watched as Mia left, then his eyes averted to Mr. Beardsley who was standing in an aisle. "What are you doing hiding there?"

"Watching you and Mia." The elderly man walked toward the librarian. "Are you setting your sights on her now?"

"What?!" Ethan shook his head. "Me and Mia no way." Ethan had to admit that Mia was a beautiful and charming woman, yet she wasn't his type. "Mia and I are friends, nothing else."

"Good, because you…"

"Mr. Beardsley, please don't."

"I'm saying you need to give Daisy another chance."

"She'll be much happier with Brock."

"I don't think so." If what the old man heard is correct, then Daisy was involved with a womanizer. "You're the right guy for her."

Ethan wanted to reply, but he shut his mouth when he saw Daisy coming in. "Not another word about this," he told Mr. Beardsley before greeting Daisy.

***

"I loved the story," Daisy started the discussion. "Patterson has become my favorite suspense author. This is another masterpiece. The book kept me on the edge of my seat from beginning to end."

"I have to disagree, Daisy." Mrs. Davenport, an elderly woman replied. "The ending to me was anticlimatic. Also, can we talk about the detective. I thought he was too arrogant."

"But that's what made him so great." Cameron Ashby paused to take a bite of his eclair. As one of the town's hairdressers, Cameron's flair for beauty was as famous as his love for sweets and books. "As a reader, I love my heroes to be tough and maybe a little cocky. Out of all the characters, I thought the detective was the best and he's the reason I kept reading."

Mr. Beardsley adjusted his glasses as his turn to speak came up. "Cameron, I agree with you about the detective." Cameron waved his hand in a thank you gesture.

"Was the detective a little arrogant? Absolutely. But that's the way most of these law characters are portrayed onscreen." He took a sip of tea before moving on to the next topic. "As for the story, there were some suspenseful moments. But I figured out the killer long before it was revealed. That's the way things are sometimes people are blind to the obvious."

Ethan shifted in his seat as he noticed Mr. Beardsley looking in his direction. The last comment was directed more at Ethan's love life than the book.

"What did you think Ethan?" asked Daisy, who was seated near him.

Ethan cleared his throat as he collected his thoughts. "Everyone made valid points. Personally...I liked the detective. He was a tough guy which is what everyone looks for in a hero." Ethan looked at Daisy from the corner of his eye. "Yet, there were parts where he showed his sensitive side, something that most people tend to overlook."

For the next thirty minutes, the group discussed the pros and cons of the books. At the end fo the meeting, they voted to read Janet Evanovich's Stephanie Plum series for their next pick. Daisy was chatting with Mrs. Davenport as Ethan and Cameron made small talk.

"I'm looking forward to the Stephanie Plum book. That's been on my to-be-read list for a while."

"Janet Evanovich is a good author."

"I can't wait to discuss it at the next meeting." Cameron glanced at his phone. "I must be going. Thanks again for another awesome book club." Cameron snatched one last éclair for the road, then said his goodbyes to the other members.

Ethan began cleaning up the area when Mr. Beardsley approached him.

"Now's your chance, boy." Mr. Beardsley glanced toward Daisy who was finishing her chat with Mrs. Davenport.

"Mr. Beardsley, I thought I told you to drop the subject."

"Not until you tell Daisy how you feel. You can't keep you feelings bottled up. It'll eat you up inside."

"I'm not going to do anything to interfere with her and Brock."

"You don't know for certain that she wants that jock. She wants you, I know it."

"Well, your intuition is off."

In the distance, Daisy's attention shifted from Mrs. Davenport's talk about her two cats to Ethan and Mr. Beardsley. The men were engaged in what appeared to be a serious conversation, one that had Ethan annoyed. Ethan and Mr. Beardsley got along fine, so it was unusual to see Ethan upset with the elderly man. Watching their interaction caused Daisy's concern for Ethan skyrocketed. She didn't know what had gotten into Ethan, he was a calm person, but here lately he seemed perturbed.

"Well, I must skedaddle. My cats will go crazy if they don't have their bedtime treats."

"Alright, Mrs. Davenport. You have a good evening."

"You too, Daisy."

Daisy's gaze wandered from Mrs. Davenport to Ethan and Mr. Beardsley. Ethan's annoyance seemed to wane, while Mr. Beardsley had a defeated expression.

"Mrs. Davenport, wait up." Mr. Beardsley turned away from Ethan. "I'll walk you out."

With the pair gone, Ethan and Daisy were the only ones left. When he turned around, he was surprised to find Daisy staring at him.

"Don't let me keep you if you have other plans."

"I'm not busy." Now that Daisy was alone with Ethan, she wanted to dig around to see the reason for his moodiness. "I'll help you clean up."

"That's not necessary."

"I don't mind." Daisy picked up the empty eclair box, then the paper cups.

"Daisy, I can get this. You go on home."

"Ethan, I always help tidy up after book club, it's no big deal." She reached for the tea pitcher then same time Ethan grabbed it. The container dropped onto the table sending droplets of tea on the wooden surface.

"Damn it." Ethan smacked his forehead at his foolishness.

"I've got it, Ethan." Daisy took some of the napkins and wiped the liquid. "It was an accident." She looked up at Ethan who had his back turned to her, and his head hung low. "Ethan, are you okay?"

"I'm fine, Daisy," he replied in a somber tone. "Please, go home. I'll take care of the mess. It was my fault."

Daisy walked to Ethan and gently placed her hand on his shoulder. "Ethan, what's wrong?"

"Nothing's wrong."

"Yes, there is." In all the years, she knew Ethan she could tell when he wasn't himself. "You've been acting odd. I saw you earlier having an argument with Mr. Beardsley."

"I'm having a bad day, that's all."

Daisy still wasn't buying his excuse. "Well, I think you've been having a couple of bad days. It all started on the night of the reunion when you abruptly left. Then the next day at the shop you couldn't get away..." It dawned on Daisy the reason for Ethan's change in attitude. She couldn't believe she didn't see the signs earlier. "Ethan, are you..."

He slowly turned toward Daisy, his eyes were filled with affection as he decided to come clean. "I love you, Daisy."

She felt the wind knocked out of her by Ethan's confession.

"I've had a crush on you since high-school, but I was too shy to say anything." He crossed his arms in front of his chest as if he was protecting his heart. "Mr. Beardsley convinced me to tell you. I was going to...the night of the reunion."

Daisy's heart swelled at the thought. She recalled their slow dance and how he was about to say something until..."Brock's arrival changed everything."

Ethan nodded. "He's a great guy and I can see why you like him."

Daisy tried to speak, but Ethan beat her to the punch.

"You're my...*friend*, Daisy. I want you to be happy." Ethan felt his throat tightening as he let out all his pent up emotions. "Brock's a great guy. I'm sure he...he can give you the life you deserve."

***

Twenty minutes later, Daisy was pulling up outside Jennifer's house. After Ethan's revelation, Daisy texted Jennifer for a girl talk. Sensing the urgency in Daisy's message, Jennifer realized a face-to-face meeting would be better than a phone chat.

Daisy walked up to the porch and heard a loud commotion inside. Jennifer swung open the door, her face and hair in a state of disarray. In the background, she saw Ryan, dressed in Spiderman pajamas running amok.

"If this is a bad time, we can…"

"No, come in." Jennifer motioned for her to enter. "Please, excuse the chaos. A certain little boy doesn't want to go to bed."

She looked at her son who was pretending to be an airplane.

"Charlie, honey, can you come get Ryan?"

A few seconds later Charlie came hobbling downstairs, cursing whoever invented Legos. "Hi Daisy." He nodded as he staggered toward his son. "Ryan, come on, it's time for bed." Ryan continued making engine noises as he twirled.

With his foot throbbing, Charlie didn't have time for his son's antics. He whistled causing Ryan to stop in mid spin. "It's time for bed, mister."

Ryan lowered his arms and stared at his dad. Daisy wondered if Ryan was going to throw a tantrum. Whenever he was out in public, he was well-behaved, but Jennifer said at home he was a bit wilder.

The father and son locked eyes, neither moving or saying a word. Daisy and Jennifer braced themselves for Ryan to scream and go back to running amok. But to their surprise, Ryan jumped into his dad's arms.

"Can I have two stories tonight?"

"We'll see, buddy. Say good night to mom and aunt Daisy."

"Good night mom, good night aunt Daisy." Ryan blew them a kiss as Charlie carried him upstairs.

Daisy looked at Jennifer in awe. "How did he…"

"He's got a gift when it comes to kids." Jennifer shrugged. She dreaded what it'd be like when Ryan hit his teen years. But when that time came, she'd let Charlie deal with it. "Enough about kids, let's talk about you." Jennifer gestured to the kitchen.

"Does this call for ice cream or wine?"

"Wine, definitely." Every woman knew that wine was the drink of choice when going through a dilemma.

Jennifer fetched two glasses and a bottle of red wine, then sat beside Daisy at the kitchen island. "Tell me what happened. Your text said it was important."

Daisy couldn't wrap her head around Ethan's confession and she didn't know how Jennifer would take it. Instead of beating around the topic, she was blunt. "Ethan's in love with me."

Caught off guard by Daisy's revelation, Jennifer spilled a droplet of wine on the oak counter. She arose to fetch a paper towel, then returned to clean the mess. "He finally told you."

Daisy's mouth drooped as she arched an eyebrow. "You knew?"

"He didn't tell me." She wiped the red liquid, then tossed the towel in the trash. "But I sensed it. I could tell he liked you ever since we were kids."

"Why didn't you tell me?"

"It was Ethan's secret to tell, not mine." Jennifer pressed a hand to her chest. "Besides, I thought you knew."

"No, I never suspected Ethan loved me."

Jennifer gave Daisy a sideways glance before taking a sip of wine. "How could you not have known? The signs were there."

Daisy reflected on her and Ethan's friendship, trying to decipher the clues. They had similar interests and hung out, all the typical stuff friends do. Although when they did hang out, Daisy had to twist Ethan's arm to convince him to go out. The only time he initiated an invitation is when he asked her to prom. Daisy recalled that night dancing with Ethan who was happy, yet nervous, the same...the same way he acted the night of the reunion. The night he was going to tell her he loved her.

"I'm such an idiot." Daisy slapped her forehead. "The signs were there all along and I didn't notice."

"It takes people a while to figure it out." Jennifer swirled the wine in her glass. "The million dollar question is how do you feel about Ethan?"

"Ethan's a good guy and a great friend. We have a lot of the same interests. We both love books and have enormous sweet tooths." Daisy laughed at the many times she had Ethan taste test her concoctions. "He's always been there for me through good times and bad. Whenever I have a lousy day, he brightens it."

Daisy recalled all the times she confided in Ethan. In school, she expressed her worries that she'd fail a test or if being a baker was the right career path for her. *"Everything will work out. Stop worrying so much."* That would always be his reply. If it hadn't been for Ethan she never would've followed her dream of opening the donut shop. When doubts about the business crept in, Ethan stepped in with a pep talk.

"This is a big opportunity, Daisy. There's no telling if you'll ever get another chance like this. Do you really want to give up your dream because of fear?"

Ethan was a huge part of Daisy's life and she couldn't imagine it without him. As she thought about all of Ethan's positive attributes, her heart swelled and a smile formed. It was at that moment she realized her true feelings. She glanced at Jennifer, who nodded her approval. "I'm in love with Ethan."

"Well, then go tell him." Jennifer nudged Daisy's shoulder.

"Are you crazy? It's late, I can't do it now."

"You're not chickening out are you?"

Daisy chewed her bottom lip. She loved Ethan, yet she was nervous about pursuing a relationship. "What if things don't work out? What if this ruins our relationship?"

Jennifer gulped the rest of her wine, then reached for Daisy's hands. "You can't let fear keep you experiencing love. If you and Ethan are meant to be, you're meant to be. If not, you're both mature adults and will handle this in a civilized manner."

Daisy thought about Jennifer's advice. Ethan took a chance by admitting his feelings, now it was time for her to do the same.

***

The next morning, Daisy awoke with a smile on her face as she planned the next step in her future. After her talk with Jennifer, Daisy knew Ethan was the man she loved. All this time her feelings for him were hidden, but his confession had her reflecting on their relationship. It was a big risk taking their friendship to a romantic level. But that was part of life's journey.

Daisy knew she had to tell Ethan had she felt, but first she had business to attend to. The door to the donut shop opened, and Brittany, Daisy's assistant, entered with her phone in her hand.

Daisy shook her hand. Like all young girls, Brittany's eyes stayed glued to that cell phone. "Would it kill you to put that thing down once in a while?"

Brittany looked up from the screen. "Sorry, boss. I'm checking out the latest gossip about Brock Tate."

The mention of his name perked up Daisy. "What's going on with Brock?"

"He went out to dinner with Mia Pearson. Someone posted a photo of them at The Dragon Palace." Brittany held her phone out for Daisy to see. The screen showed Brock and Mia looking cozy as the dined on teriyaki chicken. Daisy felt nothing as she stared at the picture of the couple. Well, that wasn't true, she was happy because this meant Mia wouldn't be after Ethan.

"It's pretty surprising."

"I'll say it is. I heard he was flirting with Candice Harvey a few nights ago."

Daisy blew an internal sigh of relief that her interactions with Brock haven't made the rounds. The last thing she wanted was for the news to get back to Ethan and ruin any chance she had with him.

***

Fresh baked donuts filled the dining area as Daisy flipped the sign to Open. Looking out the window, she spotted Mr. Beardsley's walking down the sidewalk. She waved, then opened the door as he neared the shop.

"You're up bright and early today."

"You know what they say, the early bird gets the worm." Mr. Beardsley strutted into the shop with an extra pep in his step.

"But in my case, it's donuts."

"I've got a whole case filled with hot and fresh donuts, so take your pick." Daisy returned behind the counter as Mr. Beardsley eyed the pastries.

"I'll take a box of three glazed donuts and three chocolates."

"Coming right up." Daisy lined the pink boxes with wax paper, then filled it with Mr. Beardsley's order. "Will there be anything else for you?"

He held his Newsboy cap in his wrinkled hands as he contemplated whether to broach a certain topic. He knew he should stay out of their personal business, but he didn't want Ethan and Daisy to regret missing out on a chance at happiness. "Daisy, we need to talk about Ethan."

She placed the box on top of the case, then leaned across the counter.

"I shouldn't be telling you this and it's best if it came from Ethan, but he—"

"He's in love with me."

The elderly man's eyes widened at Daisy's response. "He told you."

"Yes, he told me last night."

He was relieved Ethan finally admitted his feelings. Now the big question remained. "How do you feel about him?" She blushed and bowed her head.

"I knew it." Mr. Beardsley snapped his fingers. "You can't fool this old geezer." He tugged on his shirt collar as a symbol of proudness that his mind was still sharp. "Daisy, I wish you and

Ethan all the happiness in the world. If anybody deserves love, it's you two kids."

Daisy let Mr. Beardsley continue rambling, she didn't have the heart to let him know that she and Ethan weren't officially a couple. She hoped Ethan loved her gesture she had planned. But deep inside she worried that he might change his mind. What if he decides he doesn't love me? What if this ends our friendship?

"Relationships aren't easy. But as long as you love each other and committed, you can work through any problem."

The ringing of the bell drew Daisy and Mr. Beardsley's attention toward the door. Brock came in dressed to the nines in a gray suit.

"As I was saying..." Mr. Beardsley turned his attention back to Daisy, and lowered his voice to a whisper. "You can survive any problem, including this bozo."

Daisy gave Mr. Beardsley an admonishing look and he apologetically shrugged.

"Good morning Daisy." Brock strode toward the counter.

"And good morning to you, Mr. Beardsley." "Brock." He gave him a courtesy nod.

"I'm finishing up Mr. Beardsley's order, I'll be with you in a second, Brock." Daisy rang up the purchase, then bid farewell to Mr. Beardsley.

On his way out Mr. Beardsley smiled at Brock, then secretly shot him the evil eye while he wasn't looking.

"He's a weird old man."

"Mr. Beardsley? Nah. He's a sweet man, once you get to know him better." Daisy straightened a stack of business cards near the cash register. "What can I get for you? I have glazed donuts, eclairs, crullers."

"Daisy, we need to talk."

She looked up at Brock, trying to get a read on his expression. The tension in his jaw and the way his eyebrows knitted together indicated nervousness. Daisy came out from behind the counter and into the dining area. Pulling out a chair, Daisy gestured for Brock to take a seat.

Trepidation filled Brock as he rubbed the back of his neck. "I apologize for not coming by. I've been busy."

"So I've heard." Daisy twirled her ponytail as she watched Brock's expression turn sheepish.

"I guess you've heard…"

"Yeah, I know about you flirting with Candice. And your date with Mia."

"Daisy, I can explain."

"Brock, there's no need to."

"I'm so sorry, Daisy. I know you're upset…"

"Brock, please, can I say something." She held up her palm to stop his rambling. Once he quieted, Daisy pondered the best way to tell Brock they couldn't be a couple. She could call him a jerk for womanizing, but she decided to take the high road. "You're a great guy, Brock. I've enjoyed the brief time we've spent together. But we're never going to work as a couple."

Daisy watched as Brock's face drooped, if she had to guess this was probably the first time a woman turned him down.

"If this is about Candice and Mia, let me explain. Candice was the one flirting with me the night at the bar. As for Mia, she invited me to dinner as a thank-you for speaking at the school."

From the corner of her eye, Daisy saw Brock wipe his hand on his pants leg. "Brock, this isn't about them. It's about us.

The truth is, I'm not in love with you Brock."

His eyes widened as he leaned back in his chair, it was like the wind was knocked out of him. "So you're…"

"There's no spark between us." She ran her hand across the smooth white surface of the table. "Besides, another man has my heart."

"Wait." He held up his fingers as he tried to comprehend the last sentence. "Do you have a boyfriend?"

"No, but there is a special guy in my life and I'm hoping to make things official."

Brock was blown away by the news, but in hindsight he knew Daisy was right about them. Although he liked Daisy, they were complete opposites. She was a small town girl and she wouldn't be comfortable with his big city lifestyle.

"I appreciate you being honest with me, Daisy."

"I should've come clean sooner, but I didn't realize my feelings for my fri..for this guy until yesterday."

The light bulb went off in Brock's head with Daisy's slip up. He knew Ethan was her special man was and he felt guilty for swooping in on Daisy. "Well, this guy is one lucky fellow. I hope you and *him* will be happy."

"Thank you, Brock." Daisy smiled with relief that her and Brock's 'break up' went smoothly.

"I better get going. I have stuff to do before my flight." Brock arose from his chair, he went to hug Daisy, but halted. When she nodded her approval, he embraced her. "Thanks for everything."

"The next time you're in Danburg, stop by the shop. I'll give you a discount."

"I'm going to hold you to that promise." Brock checked the time on his phone. "I hate to run, but..."

"I understand. Good luck with everything." Daisy stuffed her hands into her jeans pockets as she watched Brock walk toward the exit. "Oh, and Brock...I hope you'll find the right woman."

"I will, Daisy. Don't worry."

"Goodbye, Brock."

"Goodbye, Daisy." He gave her a salute before walking out of the shop and out of Danburg.

Daisy turned to see Brittany poking her head out of the kitchen. The young woman's mouth dropped open as she eyed incredulously.

"Did you turn down Brock Tate?"

"Yes, I did."

"Girl, you are crazy."

"No, I know exactly what I'm doing."

***

Darkness began to fall on Danburg as Ethan prepared to close for the night. Normally, the library made him happy, but now it served as a painful reminder from last night. Ethan kept replaying every detail in his head, everything from his "I love you" to Daisy's astonished expression. His declaration left her speechless, and he left the room to compose himself, but when he returned Daisy was gone.

I blew it. I scared Daisy away and I might have ended our friendship. Ethan knew he and Daisy had to discuss their situation. But right now, he thought the best thing was to give her time and space.

As the last patron left, Ethan locked up, then began the routine check. He shut down the computers and did a run-through to make sure the area was tidy. A knock at the door echoed through the building causing Ethan to halt in his tracks. The sign out front had the hours of operation and everyone in Danburg knew the library closed at seven, so who could it be.

Ethan cautiously walked toward the door as another knock sounded. Nearing the entrance, Ethan peeped through the windows, and to his surprise, Daisy stood outside, holding a donut box. He leaned against the wall and took a deep breath. Mustering up courage, Ethan opened the door, ready to learn of his and Daisy's future.

"Daisy, I wasn't expecting you."

"Well, I saw your car still here and wanted to catch you before you left." Daisy twisted the tip of her ballet flat into the concrete.

"May I come in?"

He stepped aside for her to enter. Daisy set the box on a table and tapped her nails on the wood. She had everything planned out in her head, but when it came to executing it, her nerves made it difficult.

"This couldn't wait another minute." Daisy turned toward Ethan. "We need to talk about last night."

"Daisy, I'm so…"

"Don't apologize." She didn't want him to feel guilty for expressing his feelings. "I would like to know why you didn't tell me sooner."

"I was nervous." Ethan rubbed the back of his neck. "I was known as the geek in school, while you were a smart and pretty girl, above my league. Even though I've grown, I still view myself as that shy, self-conscious guy who is passed over for someone else."

"Ethan, you shouldn't sell yourself short." Daisy crossed her ankles while leaning against the table. "You're a handsome, smart, and caring person. Any woman would be lucky to have you. But I'm glad nobody's snatched you up."

Ethan did a double take and tapped his ear to make sure he heard the last sentence correctly. It almost sounded like Daisy was admitting she had feelings for him.

"I'm sorry for running out last night." She tucked a strand of hair behind her ear. "I was overwhelmed and needed to clear my head."

"I did catch you off guard by blurting it out. It was completely different from the romantic plan I originally had in mind."

Daisy grimaced as she recalled her behavior at the reunion. "I apologize for ditching you that night. I was caught up in the moment of Brock and his celebrity status."

"Speaking of Brock, are you…"

"I have no romantic interest in Brock if that's what you're asking."

Relief swept over Ethan's body as he tried to hide his smile.

"Last night, I was doing a lot of thinking about us." Daisy gestured between her and Ethan. "We have a special bond, one that's been going strong for fifteen years. We bring out the best in each other. I've taught you to be more outgoing and you offered encouragement whenever I faced a challenge."

"That's what friends are for."

"You're more than that." Daisy reached for his hand and pulled him closer. "I love you, Ethan."

This time it was Ethan's turn to be left speechless. *Is this for real? This isn't a dream is it?* The caress of Daisy's fingers against his palm proved the moment was genuine.

"Deep down my feelings for you were always there. But it wasn't until last night that I finally realized I love you." Her hazel eyes gazed up at him adoringly. "You're an important part of my life and I'm ready for you to have a bigger role."

"Are you ready to take our friendship to the next level?" "I am if you are."

Ethan took Daisy in his arms and ran his fingers delicately from her temple to her jaw. Daisy was always a beautiful woman, but she never looked more radiant than she was in his arms. Titling her chin toward him, Ethan pressed his lips against hers. Tingles coursed through Ethan's body as he felt Daisy relax against his embrace.

Her legs wobbled as Ethan intensified the kiss and caressed her hair. One hand was pressed against Ethan's back, while the other braced the table. The pads of her fingers skidded across the smooth surface before hitting a...a box.

My gift. Daisy was so caught up in the moment, she forgot about her surprise for Ethan. Breaking away from the liplock, Daisy retrieved the box, which was mere inches from landing on the floor.

"What's in the box?"

"This is a special occasion, so it calls for a special treat." Daisy opened the package to reveal heart-shaped donuts with her and Ethan's names written on it. She handed him one of the pastries with her name. "Now, you can say you have my heart."

Ethan grinned at Daisy's humor, one of the many traits he loved about her. "Should we propose a toast?"

"Don't you need champagne for that."

"Donuts work just as good."

There were no arguments from Daisy. "You do the honors."

Ethan nestled next to Daisy, who wrapped her arm around his. "Fifteen years ago when we bumped into each other in the hallway, little did we know that it was the start of a beautiful friendship." He paused to reflect on their first meeting. The rush of euphoria Ethan felt that day was the same emotions he was experiencing at this moment. "Now here we are starting a new journey together. One that I hope will be filled with lots of love and happiness."

"Hear, hear." Daisy tapped her donut against Ethan's pastry, then kissed him.

That night surrounded by the peaceful serenity of the library, Daisy and Ethan celebrated the beginning of their romance. They almost missed out on their chance at love, but with a little help from their friends, the next chapter in their love story was starting.

The End

About the Author

Carol Cassada

Carol Cassada is an author from Ringgold, VA. From an early age, Carol loved reading and a creative writing class inspired her dream of being a writer. Since beginning her writing career in 2008, Carol's released 13 books and participated in several anthologies. When she's not busy writing, she loves reading and spending time with her two dogs and cat.

Love Blooms In Cloverdale

Ireland Lorelei

Phoenix Voices Anthologies

Contents

Chapter One #

Chapter Two #

Chapter Three #

Chapter Four #

About the Author #

Chapter One

Emma's car trundled along the winding road, the GPS announcing her arrival in Cloverdale. As she approached the town's main street, a sense of nostalgia washed over her. The buildings stood proudly, their facades adorned with colorful murals and quaint storefronts. A row of vibrant maple trees lined the sidewalk, their leaves ablaze with hues of crimson and gold.

Parking her car by the sidewalk, Emma took a moment to collect herself before stepping out. The crisp autumn air embraced her as she made her way towards the diner, her aunt's establishment. The scent of freshly baked pastries wafted through the air, enticing her taste buds and quickening her pace.

With a jingle of the bell above the door, Emma entered the cozy diner. The warm, familiar aromas of coffee and comfort food enveloped her, making her feel instantly at ease. Her aunt, Martha, emerged from the bustling kitchen, her eyes widening with delight as she spotted Emma.

"Emma! My dear, you're finally here!" Martha exclaimed, her voice filled with love and excitement. She rushed forward, enveloping Emma in a tight embrace, the warmth of her aunt's presence seeping into her bones. Tears welled up in Emma's eyes as she returned the hug, feeling a deep sense of belonging.

"Oh, Aunt Martha," Emma murmured, her voice choked with emotion. "It's so good to see you."

Martha pulled back slightly, her hands cupping Emma's face. "And you, my dear. I've missed you more than words can express. Welcome home."

Home. The word resonated within Emma's heart, resonating with a sense of longing and comfort. She had spent years chasing dreams and ambitions in the bustling city, but deep down, she knew she needed a change—a place where she could reconnect with what truly mattered. Cloverdale, with its charm and simplicity, seemed to hold the answer.

As they settled into a booth near the window, Martha couldn't contain her curiosity. "Tell me everything about the big city! What made you decide to come back to Cloverdale?"

Emma's gaze softened as she looked at her aunt. "I needed a change, Aunt Martha. The fast-paced life, the constant rush and noise—it was suffocating. I longed for simplicity, for a place where I could reconnect with what truly matters. And when I thought of Cloverdale, I realized it was the perfect place to start anew."

Martha nodded, her eyes sparkling with understanding. "You've come home, my dear. This town has a way of wrapping its arms around you and never letting go."

Over cups of steaming coffee, Emma listened eagerly as Martha regaled her with tales of the town's history, its resilient residents, and the charming traditions that defined Cloverdale. The diner, she discovered, was not just a place to savor delicious meals; it was the heart and soul of the community—a gathering spot where friendships were forged and stories shared.

"And the people," Martha added, her voice filled with affection, "they will embrace you, Emma. Cloverdale is a place where everyone knows your name, where strangers become family. You'll see."

The locals trickled into the diner, their friendly banter filling the air. Martha introduced Emma to each one, their warm smiles and genuine greetings making her feel instantly welcomed. Among them was Maggie, a lifelong resident of Cloverdale.

"I've heard so much about you, Emma," Maggie said.

"I'm honored to finally meet you, Maggie," Emma replied, returning his handshake. "I've heard wonderful things about this town and its people."

Maggie smiled, "Well, we're a friendly bunch. Cloverdale may be small, but it has a big heart."

As the day unfolded, Emma felt a sense of belonging settling deep within her soul. Cloverdale, with its charm and close-knit community, had opened its arms to her, embracing her with love and acceptance. And as she looked around the bustling diner, filled with the laughter and conversations of its patrons, she knew that her journey in this town had only just begun.

Later that afternoon, Emma decided to venture out and explore the town, eager to immerse herself in the heart of Cloverdale. She walked along the main street, taking in the sights and sounds. The colorful storefronts beckoned her with their displays of local crafts and goods. The air was filled with a symphony of voices, the gentle hum of conversations, and the occasional burst of laughter.

She stepped into the charming bookstore nestled between a café and an art gallery. The shelves were lined with books of various genres, their spines worn and loved. Emma could feel the familiar excitement welling up within her as she perused the titles, her fingers tracing the embossed letters. She made a mental note to visit the bookstore often, knowing that it would become her refuge in times of solitude.

Continuing her exploration, Emma passed by the park, where children played on swings and families gathered for picnics on checkered blankets. The sound of laughter and the scent of freshly cut grass filled the air, bringing a smile to her face. It was a reminder of the simple joys that often got lost in the chaos of city life.

As the sun began to set, casting a warm golden glow over the town, Emma found herself drawn to the small river that meandered through Cloverdale. She followed the sound of rushing water until she reached a quaint wooden bridge, its weathered planks telling tales of countless footsteps that had crossed over. Leaning against the railing, Emma watched as the water danced over rocks, reflecting the vibrant hues of the sunset. In that moment, she felt a sense of peace and tranquility wash over her, the worries and stresses of the city melting away.

As darkness settled in, Emma made her way back to the diner, where Aunt Martha was still busy serving customers with her warm smile and hearty meals. The familiar aroma of home greeted Emma as she entered, and she felt a swell of gratitude for her aunt's unwavering support.

Taking a seat at the counter, Emma observed the scene before her. The laughter, the conversations, and the genuine connections being made. She knew then that she had made the right decision. Cloverdale was more than just a town—it was a place where hearts intertwined and dreams found fertile ground.

As the night wore on, Emma listened to the tales of the locals, absorbing the spirit of Cloverdale and the stories of its resilient inhabitants. She couldn't help but feel a profound sense of anticipation for the journey that lay ahead—a journey filled with love, friendship, and the possibility of finding her own sense of belonging in this charming town.

With a contented sigh, Emma glanced at Aunt Martha, who had paused for a moment to catch her breath. Their eyes met, and in that silent exchange, they understood each other completely. Cloverdale had a way of bringing people together, of healing and renewing their spirits. And for Emma, it was the beginning of a new chapter—one that would forever be etched in her heart as the time she found her place in the world.

The bustling diner, the friendly faces, the winding streets—Cloverdale had woven its magic around Emma. She knew that her decision to return to this small town was more than just a search for simplicity; it was a quest for connection and a deeper understanding of herself.

As the night wore on, the diner gradually emptied, and Aunt Martha took a moment to sit beside Emma at the counter. They exchanged a knowing smile, their bond strengthened by the shared anticipation of the days to come.

"Emma, my dear," Aunt Martha began, her voice filled with affection. "I'm thrilled that you've chosen Cloverdale as your new home. This town has a way of transforming lives, of weaving its spell on those who are open to its charm."

Emma nodded, her eyes sparkling with newfound excitement. "I can already feel it, Aunt Martha. There's something special about this place, about the people. I can't wait to get to know them better and to be a part of their stories."

Aunt Martha squeezed Emma's hand gently, her touch radiating warmth and reassurance. "You have so much to offer, my dear. Your culinary talents, your kindness, and your vibrant spirit will touch the lives of everyone you meet. Cloverdale is fortunate to have you."

As the night drew to a close, Emma bid farewell to Aunt Martha, promising to return to the diner the next morning with renewed energy and enthusiasm. Stepping out into the cool night air, she paused for a moment, taking in the twinkling stars above. The beauty of the night sky mirrored the newfound hope and excitement that filled her heart.

With a sense of anticipation, Emma continued her exploration of Cloverdale's streets. She strolled along the main avenue, past the quaint shops and boutiques that showcased the talents and craftsmanship of the town's residents. The soft glow of streetlights illuminated the cobblestone sidewalks, guiding her through the heart of the town.

She exchanged smiles and friendly greetings with the occasional passerby, feeling a growing sense of belonging with each interaction. Cloverdale was a place where people cared for one another, where kindness and genuine connections thrived. Emma couldn't help but feel inspired by the community spirit that embraced her.

As she walked, Emma's eyes were drawn to a small park nestled between two historic buildings. The park exuded tranquility, its benches inviting weary travelers to rest and reflect. She found solace beneath a towering oak tree, its branches reaching out like protective arms. Closing her eyes, she listened to the soft rustling of leaves, allowing herself to be present in the moment, to soak in the energy of Cloverdale.

With each passing minute, Emma felt a deep connection forming between her and the town. Cloverdale whispered its secrets to her, its history and stories carried on the gentle breeze. The town had seen its share of triumphs and tribulations, but through it all, it had persevered, its spirit unyielding.

As the night grew late, Emma made her way back to the cozy cottage Aunt Martha had prepared for her. The scent of fresh linens and the soft glow of a bedside lamp welcomed her, offering a sense of comfort and peace. Nestling into the cozy bed, she reflected on the day's events, a contented smile playing on her lips.

Cloverdale had embraced her with open arms, inviting her into its heart and weaving her into its tapestry of lives. Emma drifted into a deep slumber, her dreams filled with visions of the town and the connections she would forge in the days ahead.

Tomorrow would mark the beginning of a new chapter in Emma's life—one of growth, discovery, and the fulfillment of her dreams. With Cloverdale as her canvas and the people as her inspiration, Emma was ready to paint a beautiful story filled with love, friendship, and the joy of finding her place in this small town. As Emma's eyes closed and her breathing steadied, she knew deep in her heart that Cloverdale held the key to unlocking a chapter of her life that would forever change her. With a sense of gratitude and anticipation, she surrendered herself to the embrace of sleep, ready to wake up to a new day and the limitless possibilities that awaited her in Cloverdale.

Chapter Two

The sun rose over Cloverdale, casting a warm glow upon the town's streets. Emma woke up with a renewed sense of purpose, eager to embark on her first day at the diner. She dressed in a simple yet stylish outfit that reflected her vibrant personality and culinary prowess.

As she entered the diner, the savory aroma of freshly brewed coffee and sizzling bacon greeted her, instantly awakening her senses. The establishment hummed with energy as Aunt Martha bustled about, ensuring that everything was in order. Emma couldn't help but admire her aunt's dedication and the way she effortlessly orchestrated the bustling diner.

"Aunt Martha," Emma called out, a smile spreading across her face. "Good morning! I'm ready to dive in and learn everything there is to know about running this place."

Aunt Martha turned, a beaming smile lighting up her face. "Good morning, my dear. I'm thrilled to have you here. Today, you'll shadow me and get a feel for how things work. We'll make a great team!"

Excitement tingled in Emma's veins as she followed Aunt Martha behind the counter. The sight of the stainless steel appliances, the clinking of dishes, and the sizzle of food on the griddle filled her with a sense of belonging. This was where she was meant to be—a creator of culinary delights in the heart of Cloverdale.

The morning rush began, Emma observed Aunt Martha's skillful dance around the kitchen, multitasking with ease and grace. She marveled at her aunt's ability to remember customers' orders, their preferences, and even their personal stories. It was clear that Aunt Martha had cultivated not just a diner, but a home away from home for the people of Cloverdale.

As the morning turned into afternoon, Emma's eagerness to contribute grew stronger. Aunt Martha handed her an apron embroidered with the diner's logo, and with a proud smile, Emma tied it around her waist. She set to work assisting with food preparation, expertly dicing vegetables and assembling salads. The rhythmic clatter of knives against the cutting board became a symphony, each chop and slice a testament to her culinary skills.

Customers trickled in, their faces familiar from the previous day's introductions. Emma greeted them with a warm smile, eager to forge connections and create a welcoming atmosphere. The locals were a diverse bunch—some were farmers, others artists, and a few retired individuals who frequented the diner as their social hub.

Amidst the bustle, Emma's eyes were drawn to a familiar face sitting at the counter—a ruggedly handsome man with a disarming smile. It was Jack, the man she had met the day before. His presence exuded warmth and charm, and she couldn't help but feel a spark of curiosity.

Martha introduced Emma to Jack as he sat down at a table. He was a ruggedly handsome man with a disarming smile. He extended his hand, his touch gentle yet firm, and introduced himself.

"Morning," Jack greeted her with a friendly nod. "Seems like you're settling in well."

Emma returned his smile, her cheeks flushing slightly. "Good morning, Jack. It's a pleasure to meet you. Have you tried Aunt Martha's famous pancakes yet?"

Jack chuckled, a low and melodic sound that sent shivers down Emma's spine. "Not yet, but they're on my list. I hear they're the best in town."

As the day progressed, Emma and Jack found themselves engaged in conversations, their easy banter and shared laughter filling the air. Jack was a true embodiment of Cloverdale—a hardworking farmer with a deep appreciation for the land and its bounty. He shared stories of his family's farm, the challenges they faced, and the triumphs they celebrated.

The more Emma learned about Jack, the more captivated she became.

As the day at the diner drew to a close, the bustling atmosphere gradually subsided. Plates were cleared, coffee cups were emptied, and the final customers bid their goodbyes, leaving behind a sense of contentment in the air. Emma and Aunt Martha exchanged satisfied glances, knowing they had provided the town with a memorable dining experience.

With the last patron's departure, Emma and Aunt Martha began the process of closing up the diner. They wiped down tables, stacked chairs, and meticulously cleaned every surface. The clatter of cutlery being sorted and the sound of water running in the sink created a rhythmic symphony, a familiar routine they had perfected over the years.

Aunt Martha glanced at Emma, her eyes twinkling with pride.

"You did a fantastic job today, my dear. You're a natural."

Emma blushed, a mixture of gratitude and excitement flooding her heart. "Thank you, Aunt Martha. It's all thanks to your guidance and support. I'm grateful for this opportunity."

Aunt Martha patted Emma's hand affectionately. "The pleasure is all mine, my dear. Having you here has brought a renewed energy to the diner, and I couldn't be happier."

With the last of the cleaning completed, the two women locked up the diner, their footsteps echoing on the empty street as they made their way home. The moon cast a soft glow over Cloverdale, bathing the town in an ethereal light.

Walking side by side, Emma and Aunt Martha shared their thoughts and reflections on the day. They talked about the customers they had served, the connections they had forged, and the stories they had heard. Each encounter, no matter how brief, had left an indelible mark on their hearts.

As they reached Aunt Martha's cozy cottage, a comforting warmth enveloped them. The porch light cast a soft glow, guiding them to the front door. Inside, the aroma of a homecooked meal filled the air, a testament to Aunt Martha's dedication to nourishing both body and soul.

They settled into the kitchen, exchanging their aprons for comfortable sweaters. Emma assisted Aunt Martha in preparing dinner, their movements synchronized with a graceful rhythm. Chopping vegetables, simmering sauces, and the sound of pots and pans created a symphony of culinary delights.

In the midst of their culinary collaboration, Emma couldn't help but express her gratitude. "Aunt Martha, I want to thank you again for taking me in and giving me this opportunity. This town, the diner, and the people here—it feels like a dream come true."

Aunt Martha smiled warmly, her eyes reflecting years of wisdom and love. "Emma, my dear, you were destined to be a part of this town. Cloverdale has a way of bringing people together, and I believe you will touch the lives of many with your culinary talents and your genuine heart."

They sat down to enjoy the meal they had prepared, savoring each bite and sharing stories from their respective days. The cozy ambiance of the cottage and the laughter that filled the air were a testament to the bond they had formed—a bond that transcended the roles of aunt and niece and became a true friendship.

As the evening wore on, they retreated to the living room, settling into plush armchairs near the crackling fireplace. The soft glow of the fire danced across their faces as they sipped on cups of steaming tea, allowing a comfortable silence to envelop them.

Aunt Martha broke the silence, her voice gentle yet filled with unwavering belief. "Emma, my dear, I hope you know how proud I am of you. Your talent, your passion, and your genuine nature are gifts that will continue to shine in this town. Cloverdale is lucky to have you."

Emma's heart swelled with gratitude and a sense of purpose. As she looked around the cozy cottage, filled with love and support, she knew she had found her home in Cloverdale. With Aunt Martha by her side, guiding her and sharing in the joys and challenges that lay ahead, Emma felt a renewed determination to make the diner not just a place for delicious food, but a haven for community and connection.

As the night deepened and the crackling fire lulled them into a state of tranquility, Emma and Aunt Martha exchanged knowing glances. They understood that their journey had only just begun, and that each day in Cloverdale would be filled with surprises, laughter, and the magic of forging deep connections with the people they served.

With gratitude in their hearts, Emma and Aunt Martha retired to their respective rooms, ready to rest and recharge for the adventures that awaited them in the days to come. They drifted off to sleep, knowing that in the morning, they would awaken to a new day of possibilities and the opportunity to continue weaving the vibrant tapestry of life in Cloverdale.

Chapter Three

The next morning, as the first rays of sunlight kissed the horizon, Emma found herself eagerly anticipating the day's adventure. She had barely slept, her mind buzzing with excitement as she prepared for the much-anticipated tour of Jack's family farm.

Dressed in comfortable jeans, sturdy boots, and a plaid shirt, Emma made her way to the farm, her heart aflutter with anticipation. She arrived at the gates, where Jack stood waiting with a warm smile that sent a thrill through her.

"Good morning, Emma," Jack greeted her, his voice carrying a hint of excitement. "I'm thrilled to show you around. Welcome to our family farm."

Emma returned his smile, her eyes sparkling with curiosity. "Good morning, Jack. I can't wait to see everything and learn more about your life here."

As they walked through the farm's entrance, Emma was immediately struck by the picturesque beauty that unfolded before her. Rolling green fields stretched out as far as the eye could see, dotted with cows grazing lazily and chickens pecking at the ground. The air was filled with the sweet scent of freshly cut hay and the distant sounds of farm life.

Jack led Emma through the farm's winding paths, pointing out various crops and explaining the intricacies of their growth. He shared stories of his childhood, of spending summers working in the fields and tending to the animals. His voice was filled with a mix of nostalgia and pride, a testament to his deep connection to the land.

As they walked, Jack paused near a cluster of apple trees heavy with ripe fruit. "These apple trees have been here for generations," he said, gently plucking an apple from a branch and handing it to Emma. "They're a symbol of our family's resilience and determination. Through the seasons, we've weathered storms and celebrated bountiful harvests."

Emma took a bite of the apple, its crisp sweetness bursting on her tongue. She marveled at the flavors, knowing that they were the product of love, hard work, and the dedication of generations. It was a taste she would never forget.

Continuing their journey, Jack led Emma to the barn, where cows were peacefully grazing and contented chickens clucked happily. He introduced her to each animal, sharing their names and quirks as if they were beloved members of the family.

As they strolled through the farm, Jack's demeanor shifted slightly, and a shadow of concern crossed his face. Sensing his change in mood, Emma gently touched his arm and asked, "Is everything alright, Jack?"

Jack sighed, his eyes reflecting a mixture of determination and vulnerability. "Emma, running the farm hasn't been easy lately. We've faced challenges—rising costs, unpredictable weather, and the struggle to stay afloat amidst the changing agricultural landscape."

Emma listened attentively, her heart filled with empathy for Jack and his family. She knew all too well the hardships that came with pursuing a passion in an ever-changing world.

"I can't imagine how difficult it must be," she said softly. "But I want you to know that I'm here for you, Jack. If there's anything I can do to help, please don't hesitate to ask."

Jack's eyes met hers, gratitude shining in their depths. "Thank you, Emma. Your support means the world to me. We've been brainstorming ways to diversify our offerings, to create new revenue streams that can sustain the farm. It's a constant puzzle, but I have hope."

As they continued their tour, Jack shared his visions for the future—a farm that embraced sustainable practices, expanded its product offerings, and found creative ways to connect with the community. Emma Emma was inspired by Jack's determination and resilience. She saw the potential in his ideas and felt a deep sense of admiration for his unwavering commitment to his family's legacy. In that moment, she made a silent vow to do everything in her power to help Jack and the farm thrive.

With the tour coming to an end, Emma and Jack found themselves standing at the edge of a field, the sun casting a golden glow over the landscape. A gentle breeze rustled through the leaves, carrying with it a sense of possibility and renewal.

"Thank you for sharing this with me, Jack," Emma said, her voice filled with sincerity. "Your farm is not just a place of hard work and struggles—it's a symbol of resilience, love, and the beauty of a close-knit community. I believe in your vision, and I want to be a part of it."

Jack's eyes shimmered with a mix of gratitude and hope. "Emma, I can't express how much that means to me. To have someone who understands the challenges and still believes in the potential—it gives me strength. Together, we can overcome the obstacles and build a future that honors the land and the people who have dedicated their lives to it."

As they stood there, the weight of their shared dreams enveloped them, creating a bond that transcended words. Emma knew that this was just the beginning of their journey—a journey that would require hard work, determination, and unwavering support. But she also knew that with Jack by her side, they had the strength to face any challenge that came their way.

With a renewed sense of purpose and a shared commitment to the farm's future, Emma and Jack walked back towards the farmstead, their steps aligned in harmony. As the sun dipped below the horizon, casting a warm glow over the land, they knew that their destinies had intertwined, and they were ready to embark on a path filled with love, growth, and the promise of a flourishing farm.

The farm stood as a testament to their shared vision—a vision of cultivating not just crops, but also deep-rooted connections, sustainable practices, and a vibrant community. And as Emma looked out over the vast expanse of the farm, she couldn't help but feel a surge of excitement. Together, she and Jack would turn their dreams into reality, breathing new life into the land and creating a legacy that would endure for generations to come.

Chapter Four

Emma woke up early the next morning, her mind buzzing with excitement as she brewed her morning coffee. Today was the day she would unveil her new ideas for the diner, a culmination of weeks spent brainstorming, experimenting, and pouring her heart into her culinary creations.

As she entered the diner, a warm aroma of freshly baked goods greeted her. The clinking of cutlery and the gentle chatter of customers created a symphony that filled the air, a reminder of the vibrant community that had embraced the diner as a gathering place.

Emma approached Aunt Martha, her eyes brimming with enthusiasm. "Aunt Martha, I have some new ideas I'd love to share with you. I've been working on them tirelessly, and I believe they could take the diner to new heights."

Aunt Martha's eyes sparkled with curiosity as she wiped her hands on her apron. "I can't wait to hear what you've come up with, Emma. I've always admired your creativity and passion."

With that, Emma launched into an animated description of her new menu items—a fusion of traditional comfort food with a modern twist, using locally sourced ingredients to create dishes that would tantalize the taste buds of the diner's loyal patrons.

Aunt Martha listened attentively, her brows furrowing slightly. "Emma, these ideas sound wonderful, and I can see the passion in your eyes. But we must also consider the preferences of our regular customers. Change can sometimes be met with resistance."

Emma's heart sank at Aunt Martha's words. She had anticipated some hesitancy, but she hadn't expected such immediate resistance. Nevertheless, she was determined to make her case.

"Aunt Martha, I understand the importance of tradition and the loyalty of our customers," Emma replied earnestly. "But I believe we can strike a balance between honoring our roots and embracing innovation. These new menu items can attract a broader audience while still maintaining the heart and soul of the diner."

Aunt Martha sighed, her expression a mix of concern and contemplation. "You have a point, Emma. Perhaps we can introduce your ideas gradually, starting with a limited-time special and gauging the response. We want to ensure that we're serving dishes that resonate with our community while also

embracing fresh perspectives."

Emma's spirits lifted at Aunt Martha's compromise. It was a small step forward, but it represented a willingness to evolve and adapt. She knew that building a thriving business required not just passion, but also the ability to listen and respond to the needs of the community.

With newfound determination, Emma set to work, meticulously crafting a limited-time special that incorporated elements of her innovative menu ideas. She carefully selected ingredients, ensuring they were of the highest quality, and poured her heart into each dish she prepared.

As the lunch rush began, the diner filled with hungry patrons, their appetites piqued by the tantalizing aromas wafting from the kitchen. Emma's limited-time special took center stage on the menu board, its description capturing the attention of both regulars and newcomers.

Excitement coursed through Emma's veins as she served the first plate of her creation to a curious customer. She watched with bated breath as they took their first bite, their face transforming into a look of sheer delight. Word quickly spread, and soon the entire diner buzzed with anticipation.

However, not everyone shared in the enthusiasm. A group of regulars, known for their staunch devotion to the classic menu items, exchanged skeptical glances as they observed their fellow diners relishing Emma's culinary masterpiece. They whispered amongst themselves, their expressions reflecting a mix of resistance and loyalty to the familiar.

One of the regulars, a middle-aged man named Mr. Thompson, approached Emma with a skeptical look on his face. "Emma, what's all this fancy stuff on the menu? We come here for the classic dishes we know and love. Why do we need these newfangled creations?"

Emma met his gaze with a calm and compassionate demeanor. "Mr. Thompson, I understand your attachment to the classics, and I respect that. These new menu items are not meant to replace them but rather to offer a fresh and exciting culinary experience alongside our traditional favorites. I believe they can complement each other and attract a wider range of customers to the diner."

Mr. Thompson crossed his arms, unconvinced. "Well, I'm not sure I'm ready for all this change. I've been coming here for years, and it's always been the same. Why fix something that isn't broken?"

Emma took a deep breath, drawing upon her resilience and determination. "I hear you, Mr. Thompson. Change can be difficult, especially when it comes to something as cherished as our beloved diner. But I believe that innovation and adaptation are necessary for growth and continued success. Our goal is to preserve the spirit of the diner while introducing new flavors and experiences that can delight both our loyal patrons and new customers alike."

As Emma spoke, the tension in the air began to dissipate. Mr. Thompson's expression softened, his resistance giving way to a flicker of curiosity. "Well, I suppose I could give it a try," he admitted reluctantly. "But don't expect me to give up my old favorites."

Emma smiled warmly, appreciating his willingness to compromise. "Of course, Mr. Thompson. Your loyalty is valued, and we will always have those classics available. But who knows? You might just discover a new favorite dish that surprises and delights you."

With Mr. Thompson's cautious acceptance, the other regulars also began to warm up to the idea of trying the new menu items. As plates of Emma's creations made their way to different tables, a symphony of satisfied murmurs and delighted exclamations filled the diner. The once-skeptical regulars found themselves succumbing to the allure of Emma's innovative flavors, their taste buds ignited with newfound excitement.

Word of mouth spread like wildfire, and soon the limited-time special became a must-try sensation in Cloverdale. People from neighboring towns flocked to the diner, enticed by the combination of beloved classics and Emma's creative culinary innovations.

In the weeks that followed, Emma continued to experiment and introduce new dishes, each one met with increasing enthusiasm and appreciation. The diner became a hub of culinary exploration, where tradition and innovation coexisted harmoniously, drawing in a diverse array of customers.

As Emma glanced around the bustling diner, her heart swelled with gratitude. She had faced resistance, but through patience, understanding, and the power of her culinary creations, she had won over the hearts and taste buds of the community. Together with Aunt Martha and the support of their loyal patrons, they had proven that change, when embraced with care and respect, could lead to remarkable transformations.

The journey was far from over, but as Emma observed the smiling faces and heard the chorus of satisfied sighs, she knew they were on the right path. With determination in her eyes, she continued to push the boundaries of culinary innovation, eager to create unforgettable experiences and forge deeper connections with the people who had become her extended family in Cloverdale.

About the Author

Ireland Lorelei

She is from a small coastal town in North Carolina and currently resides in Florida. She started reading romance novels, watching soap operas and romance/drama movies with her mother as a teenager. She then started enjoying horror, mystery, and thrillers. Her imagination and creativity started her to write her own romance novels.

Ireland started writing contemporary romance and contemporary with a little erotica and spread her wings into dark romance, reverse harem and paranormal romance.

Painted Love

Mackade

Phoenix Voices Anthologies

Contents

Prologue	#
Chapter One	#
Chapter Two	#
Chapter Three	#
About the Author	#

Prologue

London, October 31st

The end was coming.

Florence Harper closed the call and slid the mobile phone into her purse.

In the dark, late afternoon, a group of underdressed young witches strolled close to the bench she sat on and walked away. Drunk already, judging by the disarticulate chuckles and screams.

Flo had never cared for Halloween or alcohol. Never had time for any of it.

The muddy water of the Thames kept flowing. Always had, always will.

Her life? That was about to change. For the better, she hoped.

Jacob had found her painting. He found Painted Love.

The last piece of her broken heart hid in a small town on the other side of the ocean, Crescent Creek. A fanciful name, even romantic, but, to Florence, it was only the place where she'd sin one last time.

Thou shalt not steal.

Oh, but she had, and she will once more.

Her grandfather had made Painted Love the day she was born. Then, every year on her birthday, he would give her what he called a piece of his own heart. Year after year, only for her. The collection stopped when Grandfather Paul had passed away shortly after her tenth birthday.

Then her long widowed mother remarried.

Flo will never know if the decision came out of pure love, loneliness, or naiveté, but she did remarry. A bastard, of course.

Within a few years he'd bet and lost all. Money, properties, art. A divorce didn't change a thing as it turned out, banks didn't care much about it when bank accounts were shared.

The bastard didn't live long.

Official cause of death: blunt trauma from a fall.

Word on the street: someone had made the fall happen. His demise was welcome, but herself, her mom, and Jacob, the bastard's only son, had to work themselves to the bone to get on their feet again.

They did, though.

Tired, depressed for all the mistakes she'd made, unable to overcome guilt, her mom managed to have a couple of quiet years before she stopped fighting and united with her father and her beloved first husband, Flo's dad.

Life went on.

Florence had become a successful photographer, Jacob a brilliant art curator.

Both remained haunted by the past. Florence couldn't forget what was taken away from her, and Jacob couldn't shake off the shame of his father's actions.

Free and successful, Florence and Jacob were never free and on a sweet British summer night, they decided to act.

She would take back those ten pieces her grandfather made for her because he loved her, and her mother lost because she'd loved the wrong man. That man's son would help her achieve justice.

The irony.

Finally, Jacob had tracked down the first painting she'd been given, the dearest to her heart, through his private channels. Flo knew better than asking the *hows* and besides, she trusted him completely. Problem was, the actual owner of the Painted Love didn't want to sell, no matter the money offered, and that meant one thing.

For one last time, she'd have to steal.

It appeared she was going to take a holiday. A vacation, as they would say in America.

She grabbed the mobile phone and started to plan.

Chapter One

Crescent Creek, FL, USA, January Madness, pure and simple.

It made no sense.

First of all, what was wrong with the weather? The calendar said January, for crying out loud. A full sun might be acceptable, but not the temperature. Her phone stated twenty-five Celsius, around seventy seven Fahrenheit. Besides the obvious wrongness, it made pulling her luggage, while carrying a backpack and the camera bag, into plain hell.

Then, the wedding madness.

Bits and pieces of crowd had started to show as Florence neared the town center–downtown. By the time she'd reached the white barriers closing up the heart of Crescent Creek, it was clear something was going on. Might be a festival, or maybe market day. She thought of every possibility except the actual one.

A wedding. To be more precise, a town wedding, as the couple she'd stopped to ask had told her. They must have been joking, what did that even mean?

Then she'd stopped a man with full mustaches and a robust old face. His reply didn't change. A woman in her thirties with a baby in a stroller confirmed it.

Someone got married and used the whole town as a venue for a wedding party everyone was invited to.

Did it mean she was crushing a wedding?

A Londoner through and through, Florence had no trouble with a crowd, but this was so... unexpected, and odd, like being to a January wedding in an overly warm and sunny Piccadilly Circus.

People completed the entire clothing style spectrum, from Sunday clothes all the way down to beach-goers and folks in shorts and flip-flops. Groups strolled in the winter sun with food in their hands, a glass, laughing, chatting, or singing.

Had her mood been lighter, she might have shot few pictures, but she was bumped against, welcomed, and even hugged, at some point. A couple of young men asked if she needed any help with her luggage, which she turned down despite wanting it. Another one offered the remaining of the drink in his glass.

Sweet, but she refused.

The closer she got to the address Mr. Beckett had emailed her, the tighter the crowd, the louder the music, and the more annoyed she became. Too little personal space, too many people and tunes, and way too much alcohol piled up over jet-lag tiredness and flight and bus grossness. Hand sanitizer could only take a girl so far, and she'd passed that stage some time ago.

She reached the address and ground her teeth to the breaking point.

A restaurant?

As far as meeting places went a restaurant was acceptable. Even more so because her future landlord's name was Scott Beckett, and the sign on top of the windows said *Scott's*. But this bloody place was closed. Utterly, utterly closed.

Taking a few long breaths that stifled the brunt of temper she grabbed her mobile phone, checked the address. The street name and number were correct. This was getting odder and more exasperating by the second.

Flo walked into the tiny alley beside the restaurant. Mr. Beckett had provided a phone number along with the address, and she punched the numbers into her mobile and waited. And waited. And waited.

New plan. She would find out where this Beckett lived, break into his home at night and beat him up for the ulcer he was giving her. It would add to her list of capital sins but who counted anymore?

Just when she'd given up having an answer, a male voice came from the other side. "Yeah?"

She pressed the mobile closer to her ear. Apparently, he too was in the town madness because the background noise was the kind she'd left in the main street. It was worse on his side, as if he stood at the core of the party, wherever that was. "Mister Beckett?"

"Yes, but probably not the one you're looking for."

Flo drew in a long breath, praying for patience. "Have I got the wrong number?"

"Nope, just the wrong guy."

The man didn't make any sense. Go figure. "I don't understand. I need to speak with Scott Beckett, please."

"That would be my brother, who's currently working. Who am I talking to?"

"Florence Harp– Hastings. Mr. Beckett and I have been in contact for renting the flat–his apartment."

The line jumbled for a moment, but when his voice came back it had cleared from the worst of the background noise. "Okay, what was that again?"

Few hours in the States and she already missed British manners. And propriety. And the cold. A rivulet of sweat ran down her temple. January heat was definitely wrong, even more so when she hadn't showered in a while. "That was me, trying to get in contact with the man who assured me he had a place for me to rent starting tonight."

"Oh, yeah. The apartment. Look, we're in the middle of a thing here, where are you?"

"At the address Mr. Beckett gave me," she said between clenched teeth, then recited the street name and number.

"You're at the restaurant. Stay right where you are, I'll be with you in ten."

Oh, gosh, what was he talking about? "I thought the flat belonged to your brother?"

"Let's say I'm his delegate for the next few weeks. Wait for me, I'm coming over."

He closed the call without waiting for an answer.

With one long intake of breath, Flo rested her back against the wall.

Stupid Crescent Creek.

The last of her grandfather's paintings could have been in a nice place like a mansion in the Tuscany hills, or in Provence. It could be in the hands of a sweet old man who would sleep while she exchanged the real painting with the fake one she had. But no. It was in a town with no sense at all, a ridiculous climate, and in the hands of some bloke named Aidan Murphy, a mysterious sculptor in his thirties.

She hated this place.

No problem, she thought trying to ease her mood. After this job, when the collection was completed, she could start thinking in terms of living, as opposed to finishing what she and Jacob started so many years before.

One last rightful heist in this messy place, then freedom.

***

"Scott!"

Of course, Rhett's loud call couldn't reach his brother, not with the stream of people around Scott's cooking station. Sous-chefs, servers, cleaners, and random people. So many random people. In the middle of it all, his brother moved with impressive speed and precision for a man his size, and at the end of a very long day. He had fed a town, after all, the apogee of months of overwork and stress.

Out of pity and brotherly love, Rhett could simply go, meet Miss What-was-her-name, and report to Scott. Maybe bring DJ, Scott's fiancé, with him for good company.

But then again, Scott was a big boy and could take a little more crap. "Yo, Scott," he shouted to overcome the noise.

His brother didn't hear him but Miss Pence did, and she started a human chain of communication that ended when Scott raised his eyes, saw him, and yelled back. "What?"

"Your tenant is here."

"What?"

"Your tenant–oh for god's sake," Rhett gave up, motioning his brother to come closer.

Scott muttered something unintelligible, possibly some horrible way to hurt him, then barked a stream of orders to the poor souls working for him, and walked over. "This better be good, Rhett. I've had it up here of this place and people. I wanna wrap it up and go home."

"You will, in a little while. Your tenant called," he said dangling Scott's phone in front of him. "You know, the woman you rented the apartment over the restaurant to."

Scott's brows crumpled. "She was due to be here the day after tomorrow."

"Well, bro, she's at the restaurant right now. She called, sounded a bit pissed when I told her I was me. She's waiting for me, but you might want to tag along."

"I really don't." Scott scratched his head. "Shit. All right. She's got ten minutes then I'm out, and she's all yours."

***

How would she recognize a stranger? How would he recognize her?

Flo figured not many people waited in front of a closed restaurant with luggage at their feet, and that man had told her to wait there, but still. Perhaps she should make a sign or something for him, or–

The two men appeared from the crowd like stars from a hero movie, at that moment when a battle or some disaster befell around them and they walk in slow motion, ridiculously handsome in various degrees of disarray.

The bigger, buffer one sported the used-to-be-clean coat of a chef at the end of a hard shift. The other man strolled down in blue suit trousers and white shirt with rolled-up sleeves. They walked with meaning, and toward her.

Part of her wanted a ready-to-use camera because, seriously, they were a sight for sore eyes. The other part of her, though, stood alert. They were closing by and the chef didn't have a welcoming smile on his face.

Flo squared her shoulders and when they were but few feet from her, wished for a drink.

Show time. "Mr. Beckett?"

The chef nodded and after shaking his hand, her gaze briefly took in the other man. It should have been only an acknowledging nod but her brain hiccupped.

Powerless against that instinct, she *looked* at him. Saw only him in the ocean of people around them.

Eyes met, held. Reality muted, fractured, and rebuilt within the space of a blink. She swore his smile faltered as if that shake-up had hit him as hard, but he recovered. "I'm Rhett," he said, shaking his head as to clear it. Then his voice steadied, his smile relaxed. "Rhett Beckett. We spoke a few minutes back?"

Nodding, she prayed her plastered smile didn't look as stupid as she felt at the moment.

Rhett. A fitting name for someone with his looks. Tall and lean, agile but strong. A tanned face enhanced the blue of his eyes, dreamy in the way of the sea on a foggy morning. Black hair trimmed and combed had started to escape in an unruly mess. Full lips that curved into a boyish smile. Sweet God.

This man had a face made for poetry, a body for dirty nights, and a voice of velvety whiskey.

She needed to slow down her heartbeat, swooning in front of a stranger was not an option.

"I'm Scott Beckett," the chef cut in. "Rhett here is my brother."

Oh, yes, Flo mused, everybody could see that in their coloring, in the bone structure. And yet, Scott projected a hard, resolute aura while Rhett was sweeter, where charm edged in sensuality.

"Weren't you supposed to be here in two days?" Scott asked her, crossing his arms over his chest.

"I had an issue with the flight, I had to reschedule," Flo replied, not missing a beat despite her voice sounded far away. Fighting the need to take another sight of Rhett was a struggle. "I wrote you an email about it a while ago."

"Ah, crap," he murmured. "I–"

A girl squirreled at Scott's side interrupting whatever he'd been about to say. She threw out an unconvinced smiled and whispered to him something Flo couldn't catch. Not good news, if the exasperated look on Scott's face was a good indicator. "I'm sorry, I got to go. This day doesn't wanna let up. Do you mind picking up from here?" Scott asked his brother before turning his attention to her. "I'm sorry, Miss..."

"Hastings. Florence Hastings."

"Right. I'm sorry for the misunderstanding, it's been crazy in the past few weeks and I may have missed the e-mail. This madness, the baby scare..." Scott shook his head. "Anyway, Rhett will follow the whole thing. Gotta run, see you later at home," he said, punching Rhett's arm as a way of goodbye. "Miss Hastings."

"Mr. Beckett."

Wasn't the day turning out to be quite the peach? Sweaty, tired, possibly homeless and with an agenda to enforce as soon as possible, now she could top it with being alone with Mr. Dreamy Stud. Well, not really alone since the entire town surrounded them, but these strangers didn't reach her, as if these people lived in another dimension while she and Rhett were on a private one.

Trying to fill the uncomfortable silence between them, one charged with unknown energy floating out of her reach, she blabbered the first thing that came to her mind. "Nice party." Lame. Oh, so lame.

Flo wished so hard for a shower, possibly cold, and a 10-hour session of sleep to recover from both the travel and this man.

Those eyes of his. The tenderness, the depth, the steady goodness. It made her want to cuddle with him, in him, close her eyes and feel him beside her. No more past to remember and avenge, no more future to put on hold. Only him.

Jesus, what was wrong with her? He was a total stranger. A man like any other.

She'd talked and seduced her way in the Russian Mafia for crying out loud, got in and out with her paint and no worse for the wear. And there she stood, squirming and fidgeting under the warmth of his gaze. Daydreaming, no less. She didn't squirm or fidget, and definitely didn't daydream. Ever.

But he stood there looking at her, saying nothing. Why wasn't he saying something? Anything? "A wedding. Or so I've been told," she added to fill the silence.

Finally, he chuckled. "It is. Kinda weird but hey, we're talking about Erik Axelsson here."

Her eyes must have grown enormous. "Erik Axelsson as in…"

"Yep, the one and only Crescent Creek's rockstar. Weird and flamboyant is the rule when it comes to him. I see you might want a bit of background info to get the whole mess," he offered.

"Please, by all means," she said honestly.

"Erik got married today and wanted it to be a town celebration," Rhett explained, looking around with a smile hovering over those sinful lips. "My brother happens to be a chef, a good one, and made it happen but in doing so, Scott lost track of a few things. It appears the email you sent is one. And that's how we're standing in front of his restaurant."

"Oh, I get it," Flo said when all the dots aligned. "I thought this was a crazy town. Now it makes sense." His soft laugh skimmed her skin, made her hold onto small talks in the hope of having more of it. "It must have been a very stressful time for him. Clearly, the wedding had to be hard work, and he mentioned a baby scare?"

He sighed, another sinful sound that topped the heat level. "There was no baby scare. DJ, my soon to be sister in law, is in her first trimester and had indigestion. Scott is an anxious control freak. Bad combo." His mobile phone rang, but he ignored it.

"I'm glad to hear. That the baby's okay, not that he's a control freak." That smile again, that tug of need. And a mental slap, because she'd come in this crazy town for a reason, and it had nothing to do with Rhett Beckett's smile. "So," she said, taking the conversation back to where it was supposed to be. "What are we going to do about the flat?"

"The flat? Oh, yeah, the apartment. It's livable, but it could do with a good cleaning as Scott hasn't lived there since summer. I can arrange something for tomorrow and give you the keys in the afternoon after we sign the paperwork. Would it work?"

Oh, every single word he said was just fine, whatever he'd actually said. South definitely warmed his speech, but words ran faster than other southern accents she'd come across, the drawl less lazy. And it lit very improper thoughts, amongst other things. Aaaand she'd fallen out of track again. Focus, Flo.

"*We* as in you and I?" God that *us* sounded good, though.

"Yes, Scott will be busy for a couple more weeks. I'll sign in his name, no problem."

Okay, so her staying in America would start with a fake signature on a contract.

Eh, who was she to judge?

"Sure, no problem. I don't have a place to stay though."

"I'm sure there's a free room at the Sunrise Inn. We can walk there, it's not far and with this mess driving is out of the equation."

Easy like a spring breeze, Rhett grabbed her suitcase handle and walked toward the sidewalk running along the marina, where fewer people made it for a more leisurely walk.

"So, Florence Hastings," he asked as they passed a cluster of cheering teenagers. "What brings you to Crescent Creek?"

Chapter Two

And, by the way, what are you doing for the rest of your life?

Probably not the right, or smart, question at the moment, Rhett figured walking by her side.

As they moved away from downtown and toward the hotel, the winter sun shone gently in the sky, quiet waves replaced the music, the occasional shouts, and laughs of the party people.

Damn, something had happened. Something unusual, mysterious, definitely shattering. His head still reeled because of it, his soul sang. And yeah, his stupid body gave him a hard time, too–pun intended. Energy had sparkled when he'd seen her, a bone-deep recognition clashing against logic or beliefs.

Rhett Andrew Beckett thought himself to be a pragmatic romantic. If his heart knew how to fly, he believed in strong foundations and a legacy that would go on and on. A family to build from the ground up, to cherish and nurture. He also believed in love at first sight with common sense and honesty. Meaning, he'd lived through a couple of big ones and, when the initial blast had settled enough, he'd seen the misplaced feelings and rectified the situation.

Most of all, he loved love. The closeness, the tenderness, the responsibilities and care for another's feelings. After many mishaps he'd learned how to keep an eye on his foolish heart. It had given him a fair share of grief growing up, but experience taught him when to let it go and when to shut it, when to use it and when timing was wrong. It had served him well and despite some scars, Rhett had dodged major heartaches.

Then, there was today. Defeating rules, ignoring good sense. Florence Hastings.

Not beautiful, but interesting. Not sweet, but graceful with hash blond hair flowing in the breeze. A smile never going all the way through, compelling you to try to and set it free. Moody eyes, gray as steel one moment, soft as clouds the next.

Full of secrets and hurt.

God, he was a sucker for hurt women.

"I'm here for work." Her hot royal British accent cut into his thoughts and saved him from mulling over feelings and the such for too long.

"Which would be..."

"Photography. I wanted to see how a winter without snow, rain, and colors other than gray feels. It will be part of an exposition next year in London."

"Then you picked the right place. Winter is a work of beauty down here."

He couldn't wait to show her around. Because okay, he might not ask her to get married in the next few instants, but he sure wanted to know Florence Hastings, see if the rip current he'd gotten caught into really existed, or if he only needed a vacation.

"How long are you planning on staying?" he added, keeping the mood nice and easy. "I'm sure you said that much to Scott, but I'm afraid we'll have to redo all the info talks."

"It's okay, no worries. I have a three-month visa. Depending on how the work goes, it can be extended for three more months."

"Not long," he mused. Regardless of what they would have together, from friendship to who knows, an expiring date shone on them. Nope, he answered his own unspoken question, it was not enough to let go. That woman kindled something, and he'd see through whatever it might be.

They walked past the Tiki Bar in front of the marina when one of her half-smiles bloomed.

"What is it?" he asked.

Florence shook her head. "It's so odd. I mean, we're in January and it's hot, the sun is crazy bright and it gives actual heat. And, that bar doesn't have walls."

"There are walls, they simply don't go all the way up to the ceiling."

She gave him an amused glance. "The roof is made of straw."

"It's thatch, which works wonders in July and it's easy to rebuild when hurricanes hit."

Florence pursed her lips. "Mh, I'm not convinced."

"Then I'll make it my job to let you see the truth."

"About straw roofs?"

"About thatch, yes."

And there it was. A full-blown smile that softened her face, brightened her eyes. Along with showing her the beauty of Tiki Bars's roofs, Rhett swore he'd do all he could to make Florence Hastings smile more often.

Side by side, they kept on walking past the marina, out from the town center chaos and into the quieter neighborhood where the Marine Wildlife Center stood, surrounded by a tiny park.

Comfortable with the silence, Rhett tried to see his town through the eyes of a stranger—a hot, intriguing, British stranger.

A couple of kids played soccer while a dad strolled along with a little girl on his shoulders. Manicured grass on one side of the sun-washed sidewalk. Sparkling blue beyond the white railing on the other. A gentle breeze combed through the palm trees. Little to no traffic. The Sunshine Inn's top floor beckoned in the distance, and Rhett knew how stunning the view would be from those rooms just as much as how Bella would spoil Florence with good southern food. He smiled, proud of calling this place home.

"You love it here," Florence said. Weird, how clearly she'd read his face.

"I do." He shrugged before adding, "It's mine."

As soon as his words were out, her smile faltered. Was it sadness? What for?

"It must be... radiant. Feeling the way you do," she said.

"I guess. Do you have your place? Somewhere you belong to?"

She cleared her throat. "I have a house. What do you do?" she asked in a rapid change of subject that told Rhett more than a million words. Florence Hastings was lonely. He knew nothing about her, but regardless of how many people she may have in her life, she was lonely. That topic, too, would have to wait for a better time to be discussed, and he answered her question.

"My family has a fruit and vegetable market, Beckett's Family Farms. I'm the manager." "That's interesting."

He laughed. "It's not. But–"

"Is yours?" she asked with a sidelong glance and a half smile. He nodded. "It's family."

***

Flo put one foot in front of the other, focused on his voice and the warmth surrounding him and not on his words.

Where was this blasted Inn? It couldn't be far away, could it?

This man was dangerous, she had to be very careful and keep the distance from him and from the longing he'd evoked like gloomy fog.

The craving was faux. The byproduct of jet-lag and and being this close to ending her quest. It had nothing to do with her life.

Damn him for yanking at all the sad, pathetic chains of her heart. A place to belong to? Checked. Family? Checked. Proud of his life? Checked.

She scored zero. Had none of them and wanted them all. "Are we there yet?" she said more abruptly then she'd intended to.

Rhett's frown came and went and he nodded, pointing to a square, pink, two-story house standing before a white bridge. "It's right there. Everything was booked for the wedding but I don't think there will be trouble for tonight."

A sport-bike cut Rhett short of whatever he was about to say. They both turned toward the bike as it stopped at their side, the engine still rumbling in the quiet. The biker, in jeans and scarred leather jacket, took off the helmet and freed a storm of black hair. "Beckett," he said.

Okay.

The stranger was, in one word, striking. Sharp green eyes, classic nose, unforgiving mouth, unkempt five o'clock shadow. He belonged to the pack of men graced with astonishing looks and a blatant sexual energy. Throw in some leather and old boots, and the deal was complete. Flo nearly rolled her eyes at the open once-over he directed her way.

Yes, he was one of *those* men, all flames and drama. So boring. "Aidan, what's up man? Are you leaving?" Rhett asked him.

"I've never come in the first place, just passing by," Aidan said in a heavy Irish accent. "Are we up for fishing? Saturday is Scott's wedding, isn't it?"

How could a man as kind as Rhett be friend with someone as obnoxious as this Aidan character? And something dancing at the edge of her mind disturbed her, frustrated her.

"Sure is. The one after I'm in, though. Shoot, forgive my manners," Rhett said turning to her with a sheepish grin.

"Florence, this is Aidan Murphy. Aidan, this is Florence Hastings." Shit.

A cold wave wiped out the monotony of the bad-boy routine, the heat of the sun, and the warmth of Rhett's presence. Flo took the hand Aidan offered with a smile just a little too bright, a heart pulsing just a little too hard. Damnation, she should have recognized him despite being exhausted and very much distracted by Rhett.

His was the face peeking from an art magazine she had hidden in her luggage.

Aidan Murphy. 29-years-old. Born in Carrick-on-Shannon, Ireland. Moved to the States at the age of twenty-one. Unmarried. Sculptor. Current owner of Painted Love, the first of the grandfather's paintings. The last one she had to steal.

She put a brake on nerves and irritation as she shook his hand. Stupid mule, if only he had accepted Jacob's offer she would have been done with this nonsense months ago. But no, he refused, said he didn't care for money, and that meant she must sweet talk her way to him. "It's a pleasure to meet you,

Mr. Murphy." "A Brit," he accused.

"An Irish."

"Miss Florence is a photographer," Rhett cut in, his palm gently touching the small of her back. The contact echoed through her whole body and she shut it. "She's going to take Scott's apartment for a while."

An elegant eyebrow rose in question. "So, you're taking a walk?"

"Scott messed things up, so she'll stay at the Inn for a couple of nights."

"Your brother needs time off, that's for sure. All right, I'll leave you two at it then. Call me when you're done with best man duties, all right?"

"Will do."

Aidan tipped his head. "Miss Hastings." And just like that, the Irish was off and she was free to breathe and let the stupid fake smile go.

"Friend of yours?" Flo asked.

"Yes, he is."

And didn't their friendship open a few new possibilities?

Trouble, also, because whatever had burst free the first time she'd laid her eyes on Rhett and messed with her brain could be dangerous in her line of work. It had never happened, anyway, but it must be, right? Losing focus and all that?

Wait a moment. Something else registered in her mind. His tone. Clipped, almost irritated. More than that, something had changed in his vibe, like he'd closed off. More formal, his warmth had frozen. And she definitely needed some rest. They'd met one hour or so before, she had no business thinking about his vibe. Jesus.

They walked the remaining of the road to the Inn in a tense silence. He held the front door open for her, but his eyes eluded hers. Until a plump woman in her fifties strode to the counter from the back and his kind-and-warm self returned. "Hello, Bella," he said.

"Rhett, sweetheart! How are you, and how's the party?"

"Scott did it, just like always. How's your son?"

"Oh, he's fine, he left yesterday. Keeps re-enlisting." She shook her coiffured blonde mane, clearing a suddenly tight voice. "Army life, right?"

Rhett reached out to take the woman's hand, held it a moment.

The comfort of the gesture, simple and heartfelt, laid on Florence like a balm even if it was not directed at her.

"We're all proud of him," he said.

We. Of course. Because he might be Bella's son, but he belonged to the town. Maybe not to the whole town but to the core of it, to the people who were born and lived all their lives here? Yes, they were all part of a big tanned clan.

Bells smiled, hitting the exact midway point between pride and sadness. "I'm a proud mama, too." She took a long breath.

"So. What can I do for you, sweetie?"

With a gesture not as fond as it could have been, he motioned her to come forward. "Miss Florence needs a room for tonight. Do you think you can help her?"

Bella looked at her in a friendly business-like way, not at all like she dealt with Rhett but hey, she was the outsider. "Of course, honey. We were all booked, with the wedding and all, but most of the guests are leaving today. If you give me an hour or so we'll have you all set."

Bella went over the business of passport and paperwork and Flo's brows furrowed when she saw Rhett's credit card on the counter. "What is that?"

"My brother screwed up, you don't have to pay for it. Actually," Rhett said on a second thought, "I shouldn't pay for it either." The smile he directed to Bella was full of mischief. "Maybe I should put the room on his card."

With the ease of someone immune to the charm, Bella scoffed and waived the idea away. "Oh, stop it, give your brother a rest, the poor man doesn't need any more trouble right now. I'm sure he's done a wonderful job today, right after the holidays and before his own wedding, no less."

Rhett rolled his eyes like only a brother could. "A real hero."

"Pardon me," Flo said when she had enough of standing there while people did things for her as if she was a dimwit. "Nobody is going to pay but me. You don't have to do this, really."

"I agree, Scott should. But he's not here so..."

"So, I will pay for my hotel room. I insist."

Judging by the further cooling down, Rhett didn't care for her stand over who should pick up the bill.

Oh, well, Rhett could get down from the overbearing gentleman train at any moment, thank you very much. She gave Bella her card. "Thank you," she said to her, then turned to Rhett. "And thank you for your help, Mr. Beckett. Should we set up a date for signing the contract tomorrow?"

"I'll have someone cleaning up the place in the morning. I get off work at around 5:30. How about I pick you up here at 6:00 and take you there? You can see the apartment and, if it's okay, we can sign the paperwork."

She straightened up a bit more. "It works for me, thanks so much."

He scribbled something on a piece of paper, handed it to her.

"If anything comes up, give me a call and we'll reschedule."

"I will surely do. I'll see you tomorrow." He nodded and left.

***

Rhett took the road back to downtown with his balled hands in his pockets. Okay, he was an asshat.

The insult didn't get down more sweetly coming from his own brain but when you're an idiot, he admitted, you must face whatever music.

A connection, he'd thought. Yeah, right.

More likely she was hot, and he was a man with a self-inflicted lacking sex life. Not because he didn't enjoy it or women, he was a big fan of both, but sex went hand in hand with feelings, and he'd had little to zero feelings for anyone in a long, long, painfully long time.

So yeah, that was all he should have read into his reaction to Miss Florence Hastings. Nothing mystical, nothing to follow up. Nothing.

It took two to tango, so if she had felt what he had, she wouldn't have reacted so strongly to Aidan.

Rhett had eyes and judgment abilities, enough to be well aware of his friend's looks and the effect he had on women. But damn it, it rubbed him the wrong way how she'd smiled to the Irish. A wonder she didn't break her stupid jaw.

Well, good riddance, he thought philosophically strolling back toward the now weaning party. It was good he'd seen it before wasting any more time over another of his heart's flight of fancy. Simply put, he gave his heart, mind, and soul to his partner and wanted the same. Anything less, to his thinking, was a misuse of emotions. Florence Hastings had shown where her preference flew, and it wasn't him.

So he would help her settle in and get over that thrilling, stupid moment when he's thought he'd found his soul mate.

With the smiling sun mocking his mood from above, Rhett trudged back to where the chaos had dimmed.

He should put some effort into making more friends. If he knew and liked most of the residents of Crescent Creek, when it came to close friends, those who *drink a beer with you when you're down, no words needed* he could count them on one hand's fingers, and spare some.

His brother was up to his neck with work. Aidan had just left. And Eva had moved to New York for a job despite swearing she'd finally settled down after the birth of her son. Damn, Rhett missed that little guy.

Alone and blue, he didn't feel like socializing any longer, so he dragged himself to his car and went home.

Chapter Three

Shitty, shitty day.

Rhett made his way through the finally clients-less aisles of his market with a sigh of relief. The activity was relentless even now – cleaning, prepping for tonight and next morning delivery, filling up the local produce room. The hustle and bustle would carry on by itself, meaning he'd already given instructions for handling it all until tomorrow.

"Heading out, boss?" Turner, a young employee, shouted to him while carrying away a pile of empty boxes. "Yes, you need anything before I go?" *Please, let it be a no.*

Rhett dreamed of going home, taking a shower, and eating, in that order. A kick-butts dinner, no way he would get by with some crap. He needed something to smooth off the day, and with *Scott's* closed, the nearest acceptable restaurant was The Charcoal, a steak house in Stuart. It meant a half hour drive, but he'd go even further for good food after a day like this.

So many thoughts kept running in his head. The talk he had to have with Tom Smith, a family friend and grower for the poor quality of his products, meaning he might have to let the man go. Also, he needed to come up with a temporary role for Barbra, way too pregnant to run around carrying boxes of fruits and vegetables. And the headache of Spring Fest, a weekend-long festival where the community met the growers. Fresh food, recipe competitions, games, and a means to bring people together while showing them where their salad came from.

It was Rhett's baby, and last year had been great but hell, it topped his already overworked schedule. He needed to find more help this time, someone who knew how The Market operated and loved planning a fun, profitable party.

"I'm gonna be off as soon as I'm done here, too." Turner threw the boxes into the huge garbage bin. "Got news on the Spring Fest?"

"Not yet." The young man was so passionate about everything involving people... The wheels in Rhett's head spun despite being bone tired. Between Turner's passion and Barbra's organized mind, he could leave the whole damn thing to them and overlook their work. A weight lifted from his mind. "Hey, Turner? How about coming in half an hour earlier tomorrow? I want to talk to you about something. Tell Barb to tag along."

"Sure," Turner said, wiping his hands on scarred jeans.

"No need to worry, it's good" Rhett added to ease the boy's suddenly tense face. "For real. Truth is, I want help with the Spring Fest. You and Barb might be able to help."

"'Course we can," Turner nodded with a jaw-breaking smile.

Rhett chuckled. "You don't even know what it is."

"We can, anyway."

"Hold on to the spirit. I'll see you tomorrow."

Happier for how things had turned for, at least, some of his trouble, Rhett got into the car more than ready for that shower.

And shut his eyes.

The contract for Scott's apartment.

Florence Hastings at 6:00.

Hell. He'd forgotten.

It was 5:40 but traffic didn't exist in Crescent Creek, which meant he wouldn't be late.

And damn him, the thought of seeing Florence despite how they had parted the day before was enticing, while it should not be. Too tired to talk himself into being cool and distant, he turned on the car and left.

***

The plush sofa in the hotel's waiting room was paradise, Flo thought while taking her mobile from the purse. She needed to get in touch with Jacob before he had an anxiety attack and flew to Crescent Creek in person.

Flo: I may have an opening.

Jacob: Quick work. Who?

Flo: Murphy's friend. He's helping me with the flat.

Jacob: An opening indeed. Why the doubt?

Flo: I wouldn't know.

Jacob: Would be a first.

Gosh, how could she compress into a text the moment when a stranger shook everything she'd always thought about attraction, about a woman's basest reaction to a man? Also, it would be the admission of an involvement she wasn't even sure existed.

Jacob: I'm waiting, sis.

Bloody hell. Okay, let's see if she could manage a half-truth. Thieves were liars, after all, and siblings lie to each other all the time. Texting an almost sincere statement to her stepbrother should not be overly complicated. Of course, she was a crappy thief and never had any real ambition for it. She wanted her paintings, full stop.

Well, whatever. She didn't have much choice but keeping it vague and hoping Jacob didn't sniff anything unusual.

Flo: I don't feel good about throwing him into the mix.

Jacob: You must make contact with the painting's owner.

Flo: I don't want the contact to be this man.

Flo could hear her brother's mind working out her words and what hid underneath them. Damn him for knowing her too well.

Jacob: No mix and match, sis. Job's a job. Heart's the heart.

Flo: I know. I'll find a way to do what I must and we'll be done with all of it.

Jacob: Be careful. I love you.

Flo: Love you too.

Flo slid the phone back into her purse and started peeking around for a magazine when Rhett walked inside.

Tired. No, more than tired, the man was exhausted. The sweet lines of his face were tight, his shirt a bit wrinkled. The smile when he saw her, though, was as warm as the sun. Either yesterday's bad mood had lifted, or fatigue had taken over.

"Florence," Rhett greeted her, taking her extended hand.

"Good afternoon."

She tilted the head, studying his eyes. "Long day or bad day?"

"A Monday after a day-long party," he said, finally releasing her hand.

"We could have done this tomorrow."

Something swirled in the dreamy blue of his eyes and he shrugged. "It's okay, I actually welcome the distraction. Did you hit the beach?"

"Yes, how...."

"You got some color on you." He touched a finger to the tip of her nose and plunked his hands in the pockets when realized his gesture. He smiled sweetly, a tad embarrassed maybe, and the tug, the magnetic need pulling toward him and into him overwhelmed her for an instant.

To get free from that ridiculous reaction, she got busy with whatever in her purse, found nothing worthy and closed it again.

She turned to grab her luggage's handle, but he beat her to it.

They both said their goodbyes to Bella and left.

Loading her only baggage into his truck was not a problem, although even parking her 8-feet Smart in the bed of his monster wouldn't be trouble. "Thanks again for doing this for me," Flo added. "You could have emailed me the contract and met me at the flat."

"I suppose I could have." He glanced her way, opened the passenger car door. "But it's not how we do things around here. Ever heard of southern hospitality, Florence?"

"I did, and thought it dead. And please, call me Flo."

"Nope. Still alive and kicking." He jogged to the other side of the truck, climbed behind the wheel. "I kind of like your name as it is, if it's all the same to you."

She could listen to his voice, to the slow rhythm of his rich words for hours, so the way he called her was so not an issue. Telling that much would definitely be TMI, so she nodded, and they left.

He pointed out shops, bakeries, and bars as they went. A story for each, a memory for each recalled in a soft drawl spiced up with humor. Such a disappointment when, all but fifteen minutes later, he parked in front of the closed restaurant.

"This is your brother's."

"Yes. He used to live upstairs, but he'd moved in with his fiancé in the summer." He led the way to the back, opened a door and then walked up a ramp of stairs. "It's quiet, despite being on top of a restaurant. All Crescent Creek's action takes place two blocks down at the Tidal Wave Brewery, which you should try. Here we are."

He opened the door to a large living room now empty.

"Scott had the walls repainted when he left," Rhett told her, walking a few steps behind her. "He went for an all-white."

"It's nice. All-white works."

"Really?" At her side now, he looked around him, pondering, before his stare went back to her. "Really?"

She had to laugh at his perplexed face. "No. God, no. I love colors and character. A house mirrors who lives in it but this is a rental, you want clean and new, no need for character."

"True," he said before pointing in front of them. "Here's the kitchen, a small bathroom down there, bedrooms this way." Flo followed him down a hallway to a bedroom. A big bedroom with a big, enticing bed in it and it took some effort keeping the eyes on the room and not on him. She was the type of woman able to read a man's brain and what she couldn't read, she felt. Rhett Beckett's mind definitely rode the same wave as hers.

"The master bathroom is over there," he said.

Wasn't it plain stupid, how a sentence about a bathroom sounded like the hottest, dirtiest, sex talk ever? His voice had dropped to a low murmur, blue eyes locked on her. That shirt would be easy to tear apart and if they didn't make it to the bed, the carpeted floor would do fine.

God.

Flo had been hot for men before, but this was ridiculous. This was almost as if she didn't have a choice but going, falling into him and everything he would give. Mind, body, and soul.

She had a work to finish, though, and it was all that mattered, all that had ever mattered. After she had the painting, then she could reassess her whole life, maybe even consider the tingling Rhett sparkled. Not now. Not yet.

For as painful and awkward as it was, she cleared her throat.

"Do you, um, know where I can buy some things? For the house? Like, sheets..." Despite her best attempt, her voice faded a bit.

"Sheets," he repeated, clearly sharing her raw craving and valiantly snapping out of it. "Yes, and... ah, hell."

"What's wrong?"

"The house is empty."

She thought about it for a moment. Of course, it was. "I'm afraid I'm not following."

"No kitchen supplies, plates or pans, nothing. No sheets."

"Yes. Again, this is a rental. I'm not crushing into someone's home, I wasn't expecting anything more than furniture. I assume Crescent Creek has department stores where I can buy what I need?"

"We do."

"Then it's okay, I'll take a look at it. If you point me the way to the bus station, it would be super."

"Yeah, about that, the only line we have runs on Market Day, which is on Saturdays."

"A taxi company?"

"John works from April to October." He shrugged. "The beauty of small towns."

"I guess I need a car, even for a few months only."

"Yeah. Here." He hunted for something in his wallet, took a business card. "Go see Rick, tell him I sent you. He's the least dishonest among the car dealers around."

"Thanks. I'll manage somehow for tonight, don't worry."

"I can take you," Rhett offered. "It's no more than a fifteen-minute drive."

Of course, he offered. Because southern hospitality was, in his words, alive and kicking, because he was a caring man and, she suspected, a fixer, and because, let's face it, he felt everything she did, and she didn't want to say goodbye just yet either.

Ah, bloody hell. Would it bring complications? Probably.

Did she care about complications? Yes.

And yet...

There was a gorgeous, fun, caring man asking to help her, why was she even questioning it? Work, with all its deception, could wait until tomorrow. Today, she would go with him and think about nothing else.

"Thank you," she said. "My pleasure."

***

Later that night.

Great, Flo thought laying in bed.

Now every time she got into bed she would think about him, with her, choosing those beddings. Who cared if he'd helped with the kitchen necessaries as well? Only his involvement with the bedroom stuff somehow got stuck in her head. Light colors were his favorite, but she'd talked him into liking a leaves pattern in a gold and lime palette - which was ridiculous. He should have no saying in which sheets she slept into. Having fun with him while buying home supplies should not enter the equation. A shame it did, and the final score was that she liked him, and honestly enjoyed spending time with Rhett.

They'd hit a grocery market after shopping for the house, and it had taken almost as long. The man's passion for food made sense since he worked with it and his brother owned a restaurant.

She sighed.

The worst part of the day had been saying goodbye.

Lame.

"I'm gonna be gone for the weekend for my brother's wedding," he said, already out of the front door. "I'll be back here on Monday in case you need something."

"I'm sure it'll be fine, thanks."

Because really, what was she supposed to say? Call me when you're back and let's get together?

Reality was, his leaving was perfect. She needed to start planning and he could be an unwelcomed distraction at this stage of the game, even if she decided to use his friendship to get closer to Aidan.

When she turned off the light and rolled on the side, with the room washed in moonlight and silence, Flo sighed. "If only you'd have been stronger," she whispered, thinking about her mom and how their world had collapsed because of a greedy, stupid man.

Would she make the same mistakes in the same circumstances? Would she trust someone so much to entitle him to ruin her life and her family's? A marriage with no trust didn't have much to stand on, Flo figured, but how blind love can make you?

She'd never know, Flo guessed as she closed her eyes. What she did know was how dangerous love could be.

...TO BE CONTINUED

About the Author

MacKade

Viv writes contemporary suspense as MacKade, and paranormal and fantasy romance as V.V. Strange.
She was born in the Italian countryside in the Langhe region, where the wine is good and Nutella flows, carried by her family's hazelnut farm.

She got out Law School alive and with an MD in comparative law. Never a lawyer, she will always be a scholar of the law.

She and her husband moved to Norwich, UK, after University. She would spend 6 amazing years there, and it's where she started dreaming of writing stories for a living.

Florida is when things started getting serious. Kids, a house, books started to add, and she made it to Amazon's 100 paid books list twice.

In her words, "I write contemporary suspense because I love the adventure, the danger, the mystery of it, and I love to see the leading couple getting out of trouble (that I put them into. Sorry, not sorry). And I write paranormal/fantasy because I love the possibilities. Also, writing new worlds is a fantastic thing to do. Besides all that, I write because I need it." So, why would you read whatever she writes?

Because her female leads are never stupid. Might be confused or scared, but never stupid, never needy. And her male leads are good guys. Might be broken and lost, maybe even rude, but they are good.

I hope you'll enjoy whatever I come up with.

Subscribe to my newsletter and get Swan's Fury FREE
https://sendfox.com/lp/m4v5gv

Find me at my V.V. Strange Author Page:https://rb.gy/8oxw0

Or my MacKade Author page https://rb.gy/tyhyes.